T0118014

The Trouble with Talent

Books by Kathy Krevat

The Trouble with Murder
The Trouble with Truth
The Trouble with Talent

The Trouble with Talent

Kathy Krevat

LYRICAL UNDERGROUND
Kensington Publishing Corp.
www.kensingtonbooks.com

To the extent that the image or images on the cover of this book depict a person or persons, such person or persons are merely models, and are not intended to portray any character or characters featured in the book.

LYRICAL UNDERGROUND BOOKS are published by

Kensington Publishing Corp.
119 West 40th Street
New York, NY 10018

Copyright © 2019 by Kathy Krevat

All rights reserved. No part of this book may be reproduced in any form or by any means without the prior written consent of the Publisher, excepting brief quotes used in reviews.

All Kensington titles, imprints, and distributed lines are available at special quantity discounts for bulk purchases for sales promotion, premiums, fund-raising, educational, or institutional use.

Special book excerpts or customized printings can also be created to fit specific needs. For details, write or phone the office of the Kensington Sales Manager: Kensington Publishing Corp., 119 West 40th Street, New York, NY 10018. Attn. Sales Department. Phone: 1-800-221-2647.

Lyrical Underground and Lyrical Underground logo Reg. US Pat. & TM Off.

First Electronic Edition: June 2019
ISBN-13: 978-1-5161-0300-0 (ebook)
ISBN-10: 1-5161-0300-9 (ebook)

First Print Edition: June 2019
ISBN-13: 978-1-5161-0303-4
ISBN-10: 1-5161-0303-3

Printed in the United States of America

This book is dedicated to my sister, Donna Lowenthal, the rock of our family who cared for our mother for ten years. You are a bright light in the world, always upbeat, giving of your time and energy, and so much fun to be around. Love you!

Acknowledgments:

I'd like to thank Jessica Faust, my awesome agent, for making my publishing dreams come true, and Tara Gavin, my wonderful editor, for making this book so much better.

This book wouldn't exist without the help of my critique group, the Denny's Chicks: Barrie Summy and Kelly Hayes. I would not be writing today if it wasn't for the gentle editing of my first critique group, Betsy, Sandy Levin and the late Elizabeth Skrezyna.

I can never express the gratitude I feel toward all of the family and friends who support my writing career:

Lee Hegarty and Don Van Riper, Manny and Sandy Krevat, Donna and Brian Lowenthal, Patty Disandro, Jim Hegarty Jr., Michael and Noelle Hegarty, Jeremy and Joclyn Krevat, Matthew and Madhavi Krevat, James Bedell, Lori and Murray Maloney, Lynne and Tom Freeley, David Kreiss and Nasim Bavar, April Lopez, Lori Morse, Simone Camilleri, Amy Bellefeuille, Sue Britt, Cathie Wier, Joanna Westreich, Susan O'Neill and the rest of the YaYa's, my Mom's Night Out group, and my book club.

A special shout out to Terrie Moran, author of the Read 'em and Eat mystery series, for her friendship and encouragement, and to Dru Ann Love for her friendship and support of the cozy mystery community.

Special thanks to the following experts for unselfishly sharing their knowledge:

Christopher Hamilton, CEO, Hamilton College Consulting – his wonderful company is nothing like the one in this book!

Andrea Overturn, oboist, and teacher, and Ben Brogadier, oboist and student, who answered many questions about music and shared their passion for playing the oboe.

Jordan Barrett, hairstylist, Salon Forte, for her salon knowledge.

Tania Yager (Twisted Heart Puppet Works) and Lynne Jennings, both from the San Diego Guild of Puppetry.

Jim Hegarty, for website and technical assistance, and for being so cool.

Katie Smith, NewRoad Foods, for her knowledge of making organic pet food.

Dr. Susan Levy, for her medical knowledge.

Judy Twigg, for being a typo-finding guru.

Any mistakes are my own!

Mountains of gratitude and love to my brilliant, beautiful and creative daughters, Devyn and Shaina Krevat, and to Lee Krevat, the love of my life!

Chapter 1

I gulped down the last of my coffee and dragged myself to the front door for the dreaded morning run, regretting my decision to get in better shape in time for the holidays. And that was before I got knee-capped by the smallest goat I'd ever seen outside of a YouTube video.

"Wha-ow!" I yelled as the little tyke with a surprisingly hard head made contact and then backed up to take another run at me.

"Stop it." I moved a few steps away and put my hand down to fend him off.

Then I noticed his accomplice, Charlie the rooster, who stared at the doorbell and back at me, as if he understood that something had gone wrong with the normal order of things. He was a Buff Laced Polish rooster, with an elaborate comb full of long feathers that fell in front of his eyes, making him look even more confused.

Before Charlie belonged to my neighbor, he had been used for psychology experiments. Now he pushed buttons wherever he could find them. One of his favorites was our doorbell, which gave him the reward of hearing a nerve-jangling rendition of "Yankee Doodle Dandy." Normally, whoever answered the door would walk him down the street back home to his farm.

The door opening before he rang the doorbell delayed him for just a moment, and then he hopped up on the planter and aimed for the button. I snagged him out of the air in mid leap. "No doorbells this early," I scolded. "Dad and Elliott are sleeping."

My cat, Trouble, was scowling at us through the kitchen window that looked out over the porch. She hated Charlie and usually made a loud fuss when he arrived. The goat must have thrown her off, because she hadn't made a sound. She was an orange tabby and the morning sun was highlighting her white chest and paws while keeping her face in the shadows, but the rooster and goat didn't even notice.

I carried Charlie down the stairs and the goat followed, hopping sideways on all four hooves and kicking his hind legs in the air. "Looks like you have a new friend," I said to Charlie as I put him down. We walked down the street in an odd parade, Charlie pecking at every speck on the ground, and the goat trying to climb everything, even making an unsuccessful attempt at the mailbox.

Then he jumped a bunch of times, twisting back and forth in a little happy goat dance that made me smile. "You are adorable!" I couldn't help but hope that it belonged to Joss Delaney. He owned the organic chicken farm at the end of the block and since we were dating, I'd be able to see this cutie-pie a lot.

We walked up to Joss's porch and I let Charlie bounce off the porch swing to get to the doorbell. We waited, six eyes on the door.

Joss smiled when he saw me and then noticed the goat. "Pegasus?"

Pegasus the goat pranced toward him a few steps then dipped his head again.

"Watch it," I said. "His head butts are lethal."

"Stop it," Joss scolded the goat, who lifted his head and danced again as if saying it had all been a big joke. "Are you okay?"

"Yeah." I reached down to scratch the goat's back and he arched up. "He just surprised me." I noticed the white spot on his side that looked just like a wing. "So you have a goat named Pegasus."

He blew out a breath. "Seems like it. Gemma gave them to Kai, totally assuming that they could stay here."

Gemma was Joss's ex-wife and his daughter Kai's mother. They'd been through a nasty divorce and came to an uneasy truce a few months before. "That's nice?" I couldn't help how my voice rose at the end to make it a question. I hurried to add, "You said 'them.' More than one?"

He pointed to the pen near the barn where I could see another adorable goat peering out from behind the open gate. "That's Percy."

"Like from the Percy Jackson books?" I guessed. Percy was smaller and fluffier than Pegasus, and he had longer ears. The black and brown spots all over his white fur resembled a jigsaw puzzle.

"Yep," Joss said. "Kai can't get enough of them."

She loved the *Percy Jackson and the Olympians* books by Rick Riordan. They were filled with mythology and adventure.

Joss grabbed my hand as we walked over to reunite the goats. "Sorry I'm so distracted. These guys just arrived yesterday." The small pen held several brightly colored wooden tables of various heights and balls of different sizes. "At least Gemma sent food and toys along with them." "Where did she get those? Goats "R" Us?" I asked just as Percy leapt onto a blue table and Pegasus followed, pushing him off the other side, only to take turns doing it again.

Joss smiled and then examined the latch as he pulled the gate shut. "Maybe Kai didn't hook it properly."

"Maybe Charlie is luring them into his life of crime as an escape artist." He pretended to frown at Charlie, and then lifted him to stare into his face. "I wouldn't put it past him." He set Charlie down in his own pen.

"I better get my run in before the farmers' market," I said. I'd loaded everything I needed, other than Trouble, into the car the night before. "Kai still sleeping?"

He nodded and pulled me close for a kiss, finally focusing those blue eyes on me.

We broke apart and I was breathing fast before I even started my run. "Still on for Tuesday?" he called after me.

"Of course." I looked back to see him watching me run down the block. I sent him a flirty wave, and then ruined it by stumbling.

Joss and I had started dating a few months before and had settled into a delightful pattern, fitting in dates during the weekends his daughter was with her mother, and when my son Elliott had rehearsals during the week. Kai had become ensnared in the same love of theater and had enjoyed watching Elliott's rehearsals and helping with costumes.

November in Sunnyside, California provided the best weather for morning exercise. The air was cool with only a hint of moisture as the sun came up, pushing the low-lying gray clouds of the marine layer back to the ocean. The hills in the distance were still uncharacteristically brown. We usually started getting rain in October, but not this year. All of Southern California was on high alert for fire danger—a bigger fear than earthquakes.

I'd taken up jogging again when I unpacked the last boxes from my dad's garage, signaling that Elliott and I were staying put.

We originally moved in with my father during his second bout of pneumonia, and I assumed we'd move back to the city once he was recovered. My dad and I butted heads for a lot of my adult life, ever since I dropped out of college when I got pregnant with Elliott. We resolved a lot of our issues and he admitted that he wanted us to stay, and I admitted that Elliott and I wanted that too.

Now we were making up for lost time.

Elliott had brought the box inside, chanting, "The last box," in the same tone as the dodo's saying "the last melon" in the *Ice Age* movie. The box contained toiletries from the back of the kitchen closet, unmatched socks, and my Weight Watchers scale.

I hadn't been to the gym in ages, but my clothes all still fit, and I kept myself busy with my job that was often physical—lifting boxes of cat food, stirring five gallon pots of Seafood Surprise in a pan the size of a manhole, and lugging around a cat carrier filled with a cat who ate very well. I'd confidently set the scale down on the kitchen floor and stepped on it.

The sound that came out of my mouth was something like "Gak!" The number on the small screen sparked my new morning routine of jogging and eating egg white omelets for breakfast.

Once my muscles loosened up and I got past the aches and pains, I went through my to-do list in my head while I ran.

I owned the Meowio Batali Gourmet Cat Food Company and we were poised to enter a new phase. Based on the success of introducing my products to the San Diego-based Twomey's Health Food Stores, I'd recently sent a business proposal to Natural-LA Grocers, which had more than fifty stores throughout Los Angeles.

It was all I could do to focus on the normal day-to-day issues instead of wondering why I hadn't heard from them yet. To keep my mind off of it, I'd gone back into product development mode, trying out new recipes and taste-testing them on Trouble. I'd learned long ago that if Trouble didn't like the food, it wouldn't sell. This last round of new product development had confirmed that she still didn't like anything with curry, but I wasn't ready to give up on a Thai-themed product.

My business had settled into a solid schedule of working in the commercial kitchen at least two mornings a week. But it left me enough time to handle the farmers' markets, as well as work on marketing and the other behind-the-scenes tasks. Meowio had grown so much in a short period of time. And it all started with Trouble.

I was just getting by as an apartment manager, collecting rent and handling issues like plumbing and lost keys for a small building in downtown San Diego, when I found Trouble abandoned in an empty apartment. She was so tiny then, too young to have been taken away from her mother, and had a lot of digestive problems. I started cooking her food and learned that some of my friends' cats had the same issues. I sold my food to more and more cat owners, eventually expanding to farmers' markets. Now Meowio Batali Gourmet Cat Food was sold all over San Diego. And soon, maybe all over Los Angeles.

It wouldn't have happened without Quincy Powell, a successful business tycoon who spent his "retirement" helping small companies get off the ground. He'd invested in my company and let me use his commercial kitchen at a heavily discounted rate. Even better, he'd brought Meowio under his benevolent umbrella—providing networking opportunities with the other companies he helped.

My head chef Zoey and her part-time assistants could handle production without me, but I needed to keep my hand in every part of the business, including managing booths at two farmers' markets a week so that I could hear firsthand what my customers wanted.

My phone rang and I realized I'd forgotten to turn it off. I checked the screen and saw that it was my friend Yollie. It must be an emergency for her to be calling this early on a Saturday. I stopped running to answer. "Hi Yollie," I wheezed out. "Everything okay?"

"Colbie! Thank God!" She sounded as breathless as I did.

"What's wrong?"

"I need to ask you a huge favor," she said. "Can you pick up Steven at his music lesson this morning? My car broke down and he has to be picked up on time."

Steven was a senior in high school, completely stressed out by the college application process. He dedicated a lot of time to practicing oboe and hoped to be accepted to a world-class music conservatory. He'd even started using his middle name of Steven years before because there was already a famous oboist with the name Jordan George.

Frankly, I thought Jordan George had more of a musician sound to it than Steven George, but at his insistence, even Yollie now called him Steven.

"What time?" I asked. "I have the farmers' market."

"Can you get there before eight?"

Who had a music lesson so early on a Saturday? "No problem."

"Oh thank goodness," she said. "You're a lifesaver."

"Can you text me the address?" I bounced a little to keep my muscles warm.

"It's a couple of miles from your house," she said. "Hold on."

I waited for her to send me the link and clicked on it. "That's not very far."

"I know this is going to sound crazy, but his teacher has a bunch of rules that I'm going to email you." Her voice was apologetic.

"Rules?"

"Yes," she said. "Like you have to stay in your car until Steven comes out. He'll get in trouble if you don't follow all of the rules."

"Okay," I said in my *I'm humoring you* voice.

She wasn't convinced. "Seriously, Colbie. This is important to Steven."

"Fine," I said. "I'll follow the rules." I rolled my eyes.

"I owe you big-time," she said. "Let me know when you have him."

I hung up and stretched my legs before looking at the document Yollie sent. First of all, the teacher's name was Benson Tadworth. No wonder he had control issues. Second, he called himself an "Oboe Master." For some reason, that triggered the Darth Vader music from *Star Wars* to play in my head. Third, the list of rules was way over the top. *Parents must arrive ten minutes early for drop-off and pick-up and must stay in their car. Payment must be on time on the first day of the month or your student will be dropped immediately. Students must practice three hours a day and document their times to the minute. Students must master reed making, practicing a minimum of one hour every day and at least fourteen hours a week.*

Geez. I'd run into control freaks like this in the junior music theater world and never knew why parents put up with them. There was always someone else who could teach the same thing and didn't have all the baggage. But Yollie was Steven's mom so she got to decide.

I jogged back home and found my dad in the kitchen pouring a cup of coffee, still in his bathrobe. Trouble meowed as soon as she saw me. The cranky look on her face said, *What took you so long?*

I told my dad about Yollie's call while I fed Trouble.

"Doesn't he drive?" my dad asked, his before-coffee crankiness coming through.

"Yeah, but they share a car." I grabbed my keys before he could get into a *kids these days* discussion. "Can you wake up Elliott while I'm gone? He has to set up for the costume committee." Elliott was the co-vice president of the middle school drama club and had volunteered to host the costume committee. For weeks, our dining room had been home to swaths of different material, four sewing machines, and various masks made out of papier-mâché.

"No pancakes?" my dad asked.

I usually made pancakes for breakfast and was planning to make them in the shape of lions in honor of Elliott's play. "Sorry! Tomorrow for sure."

"Okay," he said, disappointed.

My dad had grumbled a bit about the costume chaos, but I think he was actually pleased that Elliott was comfortable enough here to bring his friends over. I was happy that my dad had been able to see Elliott in a leadership position, something he didn't realize happened off the football field.

Elliott had been firmly against the club choosing *The Lion King* as the fall musical until my best friend Lani Nakano had volunteered to design the costumes and lead the committee. Lani had her own company called Find Your Re-Purpose. She recycled used clothes to create amazing fashions for people willing to wear wild colors and who had the money to pay for them. Elliott and the rest of the drama club had fallen in love with her concept of dark pink-spotted giraffes, purple elephants, and antelopes with daisy print fur, while the main characters would have regular costumes.

She'd also brought in the local puppetry guild to show the student actors how to make some of the more elaborate costumes come to life. They'd been teaching them how to use the puppets safely and decided that the larger animals would enter the stage from the wings and wouldn't be part of the parade down the aisles.

I'd been having nightmares about giraffe heads falling on audience members, so having experts around made me feel much better.

Elliott had become even more delighted when he was cast in the role of Zazu, the red-billed hornbill who advises the King.

With just a couple of days until dress rehearsals, Lani had scheduled a full day of costume work, and the early birds would be arriving soon.

At first, Trouble seemed to hate the mess in her kingdom, but lately, she had taken to batting around the masks. We now made sure the doors stayed closed to keep her away from wayward pins, sequins, and anything else she might decide to chew on.

I entered the address Yollie had texted me and arrived with ten minutes to spare. Unfortunately, I was beside a large hedge that ran the length of the property with no house in sight. This couldn't be right. I pulled behind a black BMW with dark tinted windows that must be as lost as I was, since the other side of the street was an empty lot.

I texted Yollie a photo of the hedge. She texted back right away. *Sorry! The GPS gets weird in that neighborhood. You're at the back of the property. Take two rights and you'll be there. You can't miss the flamingo mailbox.*

Following her directions took me right to the big pink bird with stork-like legs holding up the mailbox body and a curved head sticking out of the top. Someone really loved flamingos.

The curb had been painted green with the sign, Ten Minute Parking Zone, in white. It didn't look like the lettering of other short-term parking zones. Had Benson Tadworth painted it himself?

The house was the last one on a dead-end street. It was a one story bungalow with Old California charm, the narrow front steps leading up to the porch edged with Mexican tiles. The yard was overgrown and the garbage bin was on the curb, its open lid announcing that the garbage truck had come and gone. It was the only one on the block that hadn't been brought back to the house. My dad would've *tut-tutted* and brought it back himself, but I wasn't trying that at a stranger's house. The detached garage had been renovated, and the regular garage door for cars had been replaced by a wall with a normal door for people. It had been painted a beautiful sky blue that looked like it didn't belong with the rest of the property.

I opened the car window and could hear faint music coming from the garage. I'd become friends with Yollie a few months before but had never heard her son play the oboe. She'd talked about how much he loved it and that he hoped to study music in college. It couldn't hurt to move a little closer and listen, I told myself. I'd be back in my car in a few minutes.

Dried leaves crinkled as I approached the garage and the music slowed into a melancholy wail. Steven was so talented! I leaned against the wall, noticing the changing colors of the tall maple trees that a transplant from the East Coast must have planted ages ago.

I closed my eyes to listen, relaxing, when I heard a loud slam followed by a man screaming, "No. No. No!"

I gasped and straightened.

He continued yelling, "Are you an idiot? I've told you a million times that it's abafando. Abafando!"

I heard another slam. Had he hit Steven?

Rage boiled up and I wrenched open the door. "Stay away from him!" I yelled before seeing that Steven was totally safe, holding his oboe to his mouth. A slim man stood behind a podium with his arm out as if he'd stopped in the middle of waving it around, well out of hitting range. A large book of sheet music was on the floor in front of him. It must be the source of the loud thump.

"Get. Out." The man hunched over his wooden podium, eyes nearly popping out of his head. "You're ruining my lesson!"

Steven pointed to the door, frantically mouthing the words, "*Get out.*"

"I will not get out," I said to the teacher, who must be Benson Tadworth. "You're abusing this boy and I won't stand for it."

Benson pushed aside the strands of his long shaggy hair that had fallen across his face. He stepped from behind the podium wearing a black button-down shirt and black jeans, with black biker boots that didn't fit my image of an oboe instructor. "Who the hell are you?"

"I'm here to pick up Steven," I said.

Steven stood up. "No," he said, his voice firm. "You're early. Please wait outside."

"Steven," I said. "You don't have to take this—"

"You misunderstood. I'm fine," he said. "Wait outside."

The teacher crossed his arms, looking smug.

I stood still.

"Colbie, please." Steven's voice was thick with emotion.

The teacher turned his back, as if knowing I'd leave, and bent over to gather the music.

I couldn't resist Steven's pleading eyes, and went out the door, passing an artist's desk full of bamboo, razor blades, and tiny metal measuring tools.

I walked down the driveway and got back into the car, fighting with myself while I slammed the door shut. What the hell was going on in there? Why did Steven allow the teacher to yell at him like that? Did Yollie know? She couldn't. No mother would allow that treatment of her own kid.

The maple trees had lost their charm and I could almost sense the desperation in the music coming from the garage. Had my outburst caused it?

A minivan arrived, the sliding door opening automatically to let out a young teen girl. She smiled and waved to her mother, carrying her music case and a notebook as she made her way to the garage. I had to hold myself back from telling her mother what I'd overheard.

At exactly five minutes to eight, Steven came out. Benson stuck his head through the door, talking on his cell phone, and lifted a finger for his next student to wait.

Steven walked stiffly to my car, anger and embarrassment emanating from him in every step. He got in without looking at me and slammed the door as hard as I had. "Where's Mom?" He could barely get the words out past his clenched jaw.

"Her car broke down and she asked me to pick you up," I explained, as I pulled out and then made a U-turn to head to his house.

He didn't respond.

I sent a few glances toward him. It had been a couple of months since I'd seen him and he seemed older—taller with more definition in his face. Maybe that's what happened to teen boys at that age. "Can I ask you a question?"

He nodded, his bangs falling across his eyes. He kept his head down, maybe to avoid looking at me.

"Why do you put up with that?"

"You don't understand!" The words burst out of him. "He's a genius. I've learned so much from him in such a short time—"

I cut him off. "That's no excuse," I argued. "I'm sure there's another oboe teaching genius who wouldn't yell at you."

"That's not how it works." He raised one hand as if to pull on his hair. Then he took a deep breath and relaxed his hand. "He's the only one anywhere close to here that we can afford."

"But—"

"Stop it. Just stop." His voice was shaking but firm. "My mom has worked her butt off. *I've* worked my butt off to pay for his lessons. I will put up with anything to become a musician."

I stayed silent the rest of the way to his house.

He finally met my eyes when I stopped in front of his house. They teemed with determination. I recognized that look from Elliott when he was auditioning for a new role.

"Does your mom know?" I asked, resigned.

"Yes," he said.

"Okay," I said.

He nodded. "Thank you for the ride." He took off his seat belt and gathered his things. "Shoot."

"What?"

"I forgot my Zoom recorder," he said.

"Sorry," I said. "Do you want to go back?" I offered, even though I was worried about getting to the farmers' market in time.

He shook his head. "My mom will take me later."

Obviously he didn't trust me.

I watched him go into the cute cottage that Yollie rented, wondering what I was going to say to her. I still wasn't sure by the time I got home. A bunch of drama kids had invaded early, probably at Elliott's invitation. They were playing with the costumes but Lani would get them settled down into their tasks once she arrived.

I tried to act normal, putting out the snacks and drinks automatically. My dad must've noticed my distress. "You okay?" he asked.

I looked over my shoulder to make sure the students were occupied and told him what happened.

My dad shook his head. "Stay out of it. Steven's not a little kid. He can take care of himself."

"Stay out of what?" Elliott asked from behind me. I turned to see him holding a large empty bowl that he used to make papier-mâché.

I looked at my dad who answered for me. "Your mom heard Steven's music teacher yelling at him."

Elliott frowned. "Do you think he yells at Franny too?"

"Quincy's Franny?" I asked.

He nodded. "He told me she's taking lessons from some oboe teacher who normally only takes high school students."

Oh man. I'd forgotten all about that. Franny was Quincy Powell's granddaughter.

I knew he would not like the idea of someone yelling at his granddaughter.

"Well, she probably goes to another teacher," I reassured him but as soon as he filled up the bowl and went back to the dining room, I texted Quincy. *Does Franny take lessons from Benson Tadworth?*

Yes, he texted back. *Why?*

"It's not your business," my dad warned.

I pushed the button to call Quincy. "I have to tell him."

Trouble meowed. *Busybodies never win.*

My dad shook his head. "Don't say I didn't warn you."

Chapter 2

My cell phone buzzed the next morning as I was stirring chopped bison for a new cat food recipe that I was already pretty sure Trouble wouldn't like. But being in new product mode had me trying all kinds of strange things.

Trouble took turns sitting on her windowsill perch surveying the neighborhood and dropping down to twist around my ankles. *Finish already and let me taste test!*

Another early call? That couldn't be good. I glanced at the screen and then immediately whipped off my gloves and grabbed it. Only bad news would make my head chef Zoey call me on a Sunday.

"Zoey? What's wrong?" I asked.

"Quincy got in a fight last night!" I couldn't tell if she was proud or upset.

"What?"

"I've had like ten people text me saying they heard he was in a fight on Main Street, right in front of Happy Aprons Grocers," she said. "Like, actually punching someone."

I couldn't imagine easygoing Quincy fighting. "Who? Why?"

"Something about his granddaughter," Zoey said.

My stomach sank. "Did you talk to him?"

"I've texted him a couple of times and he hasn't responded," she said.

"Oh man," I said. "Let me try calling him." Quincy was one of the few people I knew who woke up earlier than I did.

"Then call me back and tell me what's going on!" Zoey asked.

"I will," I said and hung up before hitting the button for Quincy.

"I'm fine," he said by way of answering.

"Oh good," I said. "What happened?"

"I asked Franny if she liked her oboe teacher and she told me he was mean and she wanted to quit," he said.

Oh no. This was *so* my fault. "So what'd you do?"

"I went to his house to have a little talk with him and saw him driving away. I followed him to the grocery store."

"Happy Aprons?" I asked.

"Yes," he said. "How did you know?"

"'Cause everyone is talking about it!" My voice rose an octave.

He sighed. "Everyone should mind their own business."

"But why did you punch him?" I still couldn't believe mild-mannered Quincy could do such a thing.

"He was insulting," he said.

"Just tell me everything," I said.

"I introduced myself and told him that Franny would not be coming back," he said. "He lost his nut and yelled, 'Good riddance.'"

"Okay." I drew out the word, knowing there had to be more.

"He said that the only reason he took her as a student was because I was..."

"Rich?"

"Yes!" He sounded outraged. "And that Franny didn't have an ounce of talent and it was a waste of his time to work with her."

"Oh." I thought how I'd feel if someone said that about Elliott. "I would've punched him too."

Trouble meowed. *Me too.*

"Damn right," he said. "He went down like a sack of potatoes. Cried like a baby."

I stayed quiet for a minute. "He could sue you."

"Let him." But he sounded unsure. "Don't worry. This will blow over."

"I hope so," I said. I heard someone yelling in the background and thought I recognized his wife's voice.

"I gotta go," he muttered quietly into the phone. "See you tomorrow." He hung up.

Trouble meowed again. *It's not blowing over.*

I was about to call Zoey back to tell her what I'd learned when the front doorbell rang. I looked through the kitchen window to see who was on the front porch.

It was Yollie. Uh-oh.

I put the pan on the back burner and turned off the stove, then took a few deep breaths and answered the door.

"What did you do?" It was Yollie, angrier than I'd ever seen her. She wasn't wearing any makeup, and she had pulled her hair back into an unruly ponytail. As a hairdresser, she usually made sure to look her best in public.

"I had to tell Quincy," I said. "I didn't know he'd punch the guy."

"That *guy* is the only chance Steven has of getting into a conservatory!" she said. "You ruined that for him."

I tried to calm her down. "Yollie, Benson won't connect Quincy to Steven."

"Oh my God," she said. "Benson is not an idiot. You're publicly connected to Quincy. He's going to figure it out and then refuse to teach Steven anymore. He can't change teachers in his senior year. He's so close." She sounded like she was going to cry.

I had to try reasoning with her one more time. "But Steven is so talented. He'll get in no problem."

"You have no idea how it works!" she yelled, waving her arms around. "Steven needs Benson's recommendation or he won't even get an audition. Music is his *life!*"

Oh man. What did I do? "I didn't know," I said, my voice quiet with embarrassment. "Should I go apologize to Benson?"

"No!" she shouted.

"Okay," I said. "What can I do?"

She shook her head, taking a few breaths. "I guess an apology is worth a try. But I have to go with you to make sure you..."

Don't screw it up even more? "I understand," I said. "Should we go now?"

She looked at her watch. "It's too early to bother him."

But not too early to yell at me.

"I'll pick you up at eleven," she said. "He doesn't have students then."

"I'll be ready," I said and watched her walk stiffly back to her car.

Trouble sat in the middle of the kitchen, probably waiting impatiently for her taste, but her expression said *I told you so.*

I texted Zoey back to let her know that Quincy said he was fine and would see us tomorrow, so she wouldn't badger me for more information. Quincy would fill her in if he wanted.

She texted back. *I couldn't wait anymore and called him. It went right to voice mail. Is he mad at me?*

I texted back. *He hung up fast because his wife was yelling at him. Maybe wait a few minutes.*

She texted back a laughing emoji.

I opened the door into the dining room and saw the mayhem as a result of the previous day's costume marathon. The earlier explosion of material, paint, and glitter was beginning to come together in costumes that were approaching Lani's designs.

Lani and I had become best friends years before, when she designed costumes for Elliott's first junior theater group. I'd made the mistake of thinking that since I'd sewn one Halloween costume, I could handle being on a costume committee. Little did I know that the more experienced stage moms signed up right away to fill the volunteer slots for ushering and backstage monitoring—the costume committee required real work and long hours of measuring, fitting, sewing, and glue-gunning fake baubles onto anything from princess dresses in *Cinderella* to Egyptian tombs in *Aida*.

My dad was still sleeping and I needed advice, so I texted Lani. *You up?* *Yep*, she texted back. *Call if you want.*

I told her the whole story, grateful that she totally backed me up about confronting Benson.

"I would've punched him in the nose." Her indignation on my behalf made me feel momentarily better.

"You aren't far off." I filled her in on Quincy's one-sided fight and Yollie's visit.

She was quiet for a minute. "Oh man, that's tough," she said. "I guess you have to suck it up and apologize. I bet he'll come around if you throw around words like 'creative genius' and not understanding his 'creative process.'"

"Shoot," I said. "You're right."

"I'll be over soon to pick up a few costumes," she said. "You can practice falling on your sword."

"Have you met the goats yet?" I asked, already knowing the answer.

"No!" she said. "But I'm willing to put these costumes aside for a visit."

"Let's go see them when you get here," I said.

Ten minutes later, Lani arrived on her bright pink Schwinn cruiser with a flowered basket on the front. She bounced the bicycle up the porch steps and leaned it against the wooden rail.

"How are you going to take costumes home on that?" I asked.

She slid off her pink backpack that she'd decorated with painted flowers, and held it up in a "Ta-Da!" fashion. "They'll squish in." Then she took a deep dramatic sniff. "I smell coffee."

I reached for a Meowio travel mug with paw prints running across it from behind the rocking chair and handed it to her. "Bless you, my child," she said and took a sip. Lani suffered from chronic indigestion and her wife Piper was a pediatrician who didn't allow coffee in their house because it sometimes caused a flare-up. As a fellow caffeine addict, I understood that the risks sometimes outweighed the costs, especially where coffee was concerned.

We were on our way to the farm when we saw Joss and Kai walking toward us with the goats on leashes. The goats didn't know what to make of that, pulling this way and that, and getting the leashes tangled around their legs. Their bleating sounded like complaining today.

"That looks fun," I said when we were close enough to talk. "I never knew goats could be leash trained."

"They can," Kai said. "But it's going to take a lot of work." She looked up at her dad, as if assigning the job to him. "Did I tell you that Percy and Pegasus are Nigerian Dwarf goats? My mom thought they were Nubian goats, but they're Nigerian goats. When they get bigger, we're going to milk them and make cheese. Isn't that cool?"

It was so cute how earnest ten-year-old girls could be. "That is definitely cool. I love goat cheese."

"And they're really smart too," she said. "I'm going to teach them tricks!"

Lani dropped down to sit on the ground and both goats climbed on her. "Oof," she said, as Pegasus jumped off and caught her in the side. Then he gently butted his head against her as if to apologize. "It's okay. You're just a baby, aren't you? Trying to figure out how all of those legs work."

Percy seemed to take to the leash better. He crawled right into Lani's lap, curled up and put his head on her knee as if going to sleep.

"I think Percy needs a nap," I said, and reached down to pet him behind his floppy ears.

"He likes cozy things," Kai said. She bent over to gently scold him. "Percy, it's time to go. You need your exercise."

Kai was as cute as the goats.

* * * *

Yollie texted me right at eleven and I came outside to join her in her car, trying not to feel like a teenager who was being forced to apologize for something that was *not my fault*.

Tension seemed to radiate from Yollie's body, as if she still wasn't sure this was the right move. I didn't bother with small talk, worried that anything I said would make her blow up.

She parked in Benson's ten-minute parking zone, the car jerking to a stop as her nerves got the best of her. "Sorry," she said, and took a deep breath.

Her agitation was contagious, and I had to force my shoulders to relax as we walked up to Benson's house. Clouds had moved in, getting darker gray as the day wore on. While everyone was hoping for the first major rainfall of the season, I couldn't help but think of them as an omen. Yollie took the lead and knocked on the door. No answer. She knocked again and I felt a wave of relief when no one answered.

"Well, that's anticlimactic," I said.

She frowned.

Okay, I got it. No joking allowed. "Sorry," I said. "I'm nervous."

She didn't respond.

"Should we try the garage?" I asked.

She tipped her head, listening for music, but the garage was silent. "I guess. It doesn't seem like he's practicing."

We walked down the driveway, the scuffling of the leaves now just sounding sad. The sky blue door seemed to beckon us, like a candy house in a fairy tale.

I smelled a whiff of rotten eggs and ignored it at first. Then the scent grew too strong not to say something. "Is that gas?" I asked.

Yollie nodded. "Natural gas, right?"

We stuck our noses in the air like bloodhounds, trying to track down where it was coming from. The scent grew even stronger as we moved closer to the garage.

"Is it going to blow up?" I asked.

She looked uneasy. "The concentration has to be crazy high to do that," she said. "I called the gas company once when we had a small leak and they told me that."

We stopped and eyed each other nervously, the smell of gas a clear warning. "This seems pretty concentrated," I said, wanting to hold my nose and run away.

"What if he's in there?" she asked. "That can't be healthy."

I reached for the doorknob.

"Stop!" she said quickly. "What if the door makes a spark?"

My heart raced. "I don't think that's the way it works." I might have been trying to convince myself. "Okay." I pointed down the driveway. "You go down there and call 911. According to one online video I've seen, a cell phone can start a fire." I straightened my shoulders. "I'll go peek in there and see if he's okay." The idea of Schrödinger's cat popped into my head. Right now that blue door was Schrödinger's door. We didn't know if anyone was even inside the garage, let alone affected by the gas.

Yollie ran halfway down the driveway and pulled out her phone. After listening to the message, she clicked a button, which sounded cartoonishly loud. "Hi, I'd like to report a gas leak."

I ever so slowly turned the door knob, the creak it made sending me into a tizzy. An intense smell of gas swooshed over me as I pulled open the door. Two feet in black biker boots that I recognized were splayed on the floor. They were connected to two legs, and the rest of Benson.

"He's in here!" I said. "Hold the door for me!"

She took a few steps toward me, and then stopped to throw her phone to the ground before running back to me. She held the door open with one foot, straining to see inside. "Hurry! That gas smells awful!"

He was face down but it was definitely Benson. I grabbed him by the ankles, pulling him as fast as I could outside, his head bumping on the one step to the driveway while Yollie held the door open. I pushed aside the thought that his face would definitely be bruised.

Yollie searched for something to prop the door open, her head turning back and forth wildly, but there was nothing close enough for her to reach. She let it close and squinched up her face as it met the doorjamb. I realized I was mirroring her expression.

I breathed a sigh of relief as she came to help me. "Turn him over!" Her voice was urgent.

I followed her orders, and she grabbed him under his arms as we awkwardly made our way down the driveway. "He's bleeding!" she said.

We shuffled away from the garage as fast as we could while carrying his full weight. I made the mistake of looking down at him. His shirt was soaked with blood.

I heard sirens approaching and felt a wave of relief that everything would be okay.

Then the air around us seemed to contract and my heart stopped.

The garage blew up in a flashing burst of light and the loudest boom I'd ever heard, and the sky blue door hurtled toward us.

Chapter 3

In the movies, an explosion sends the actors flying through space with their arms and legs splayed out. This time, the hot blast sent us toward the ground in a heap of tangled limbs. My face bounced on Benson's boots and I had the strange thought that the metal buckle outline would be forever pressed into my face.

I sat up slowly and saw Yollie nearby, with a lifeless Benson in between us. She shook her head, looking as dazed as I felt.

Somehow the door had completely missed us, squeezing past like the Knight Bus in the *Harry Potter* novels and landing almost in the street. Small bits of garage debris rained down all around us.

A fire truck stopped at the end of the driveway and several firefighters raced up to help us.

"You okay?" I asked Yollie, but my voice sounded like I was underwater. She stared down at Benson. "He's dead."

I wasn't sure I heard her correctly, but I scooted crab-like a few steps back. "What?"

She pointed a shaking finger and I followed it to the small hole in the side of his neck.

* * * *

Pure chaos followed. EMTs swarmed all three of us, asking Yollie and me our names and checking our vital signs. The firefighters doused the small fire on one fragment of a wall, which was all that was left of the garage, but stayed away from the flames shooting from the open gas line.

Once they made sure Yollie and I weren't seriously injured, they moved us across the street to the waiting ambulance. I couldn't take my eyes off the scene, details cascading through my brain like a roll of photos clicking by. The pulsing vein in the forehead of the man yelling into his phone at the local utility company to turn off the gas. The acrid smell of charred wood and melting plastic. The splat of boots on the wet pavement. The iridescent whiteness of the sheet covering Benson.

Yollie and I waited in the back of the ambulance. The police officers who arrived in the first patrol car asked us if we were okay, and then moved to the body, waiting for someone further up the chain of command to take over. They placed crime scene tape to keep people a block away.

A local news van showed up and I was suddenly grateful for the distance.

My ears crackled and then seemed to release, like recovering from an airplane ride, and I could hear better. "Someone had to make that explosion happen," I said slowly, figuring it out as I spoke. "To cover up Benson's...murder."

"Oh my God," Yollie said. "Benson is dead."

"Why would someone kill an oboe teacher?" I didn't really expect her to answer.

"I have to let Steven know I'm okay," Yollie said. She felt around for her phone, but it was gone, now part of the crime scene.

I pulled mine out of my back pocket and handed it to her. When she was done, I texted my dad a cryptic message. *Had a problem at the oboe teacher's house. Will text more when I know something.*

He responded right away. *That explosion?*

Shoot. He'd already heard about it. *We're both fine but we can't leave yet. I'm on my way.*

Please just stay there and take care of Elliott and I'll keep you updated. Besides, you won't be able to get past the crime scene tape.

He sent me an emoji of an angry face, along with *Fine*, making me smile. I still couldn't get over my dad using emojis.

"I know I should feel bad about Benson," Yollie said, with a hitch in her voice. "But I can't stop thinking that now he can't help Steven get into college. He just needed a couple more months. It's like I have this selfish loop playing in my mind, over and over."

I reached out to grab her hand. "It's the adrenaline. It's making your brain think only about self-preservation."

More fire trucks arrived, probably because of the high fire danger at this time of year, and the firefighters spread out, monitoring the surrounding area.

Then a sheriff's car arrived and out stepped Detective Norma Chiron and her partner Detective Ragnor. She stopped to talk to one of the police officers before coming over to us.

I'd met Norma the first time I'd found a dead body, and I recognized that hunter's look in her eye. It didn't matter that we'd become friends since then. Both Yollie and I were in her sights as possible suspects for whatever just happened.

She walked up to us. "Are you two okay?"

She must have heard from the officer that we were cleared by the EMTs, but wanted our confirmation before questioning us.

When we both nodded, she told Yollie, "Detective Ragnor will drive you to the station and Colbie will ride with me. The patrol officer will bring your car."

We both gingerly stepped down from the ambulance. Yollie winced and I limped, the aches of being hit by an explosion making themselves felt. "Who knew being blown up could be so painful?" I asked.

Yollie gave me a grim smile and glanced over at the sheet covering Benson. "It could have been much worse."

* * * *

The only question Norma asked on the short trip to the sheriff's station was, "Are you sure you're fine?"

I nodded, feeling somewhat as if I might cry. I excused myself to the ladies' room once we got to the station and saw a bruise blooming on my cheek. For some reason, that made me tear up even more, but that stopped when Norma led me to the interrogation room. They called it a conference room, but I knew what it was.

Norma was all business. She wanted to know why I was at Benson's house with Yollie and was particularly interested in Quincy's fight, asking me in several different ways what I knew about it.

"Look," I said. "I was at one of Benson's lessons exactly one time and heard him being abusive. There has to be lots of disgruntled parents, and students too. Plus, if he's that much of a jerk to people who are paying him, how does he treat the rest of the world?"

Norma raised her eyebrows. "But we know of only one person who punched him."

"Quincy is not capable of killing someone," I said, understanding right away where she was going.

She nodded. "Tell me again why Yollie chose this time to go to Mr. Tadworth's house."

"Oh for crying out loud," I said, losing my patience. "You think Yollie did this and used me as a cover? Why would she try to save him? Believe me, she was as surprised and shocked as I was when we saw he was dead. And especially when we were almost blown up." The last two words were said very loudly.

Norma didn't let up, and once again I went through how and why we arrived at the house when we did. Then she asked for a detailed account of what I did all morning, which ended with, "And Trouble hated the bison dish."

She smiled a bit at that.

After what seemed like forever, I was allowed to leave. "Please don't discuss this with anyone, especially Quincy."

I nodded, but there was no way I was following that request.

Yollie came out of another "conference" room at the same time, and we made our way to the lobby where Steven and Joss were waiting.

I went right into Joss's arms, tears springing to my eyes, and Yollie hugged Steven tightly.

Steven just said, "Mom," in a rough voice.

Joss pulled me back to look at me, his fingers brushing my bruised cheek. "Are you okay? All your dad said was that you were near that explosion."

I shook my head. "Let's get out of here."

"Do you want a ride home?" he asked Yollie.

When she looked confused that he was offering, he explained, "I brought Steven here. I'm pretty sure they're keeping your car for a while."

Yollie's face pinched with worry. "Can you drop me off at the Rent-A-Wreck off of Main Street?" she asked. "Detective Ragnor said I'll get my car back in a day or two."

Joss kept his arm around me as we left the station, the November air chilling my arms. It seemed so weird that the sun was shining and everyone was going about their business when something so awful had happened.

The car rental office was only a few blocks away and we all stayed silent until Joss pulled up in front. I got out of the car to hug Yollie. "It'll be okay," I told her.

She nodded and we watched them go in before pulling away from the curb.

"Where's Kai?" I asked, remembering that it was Joss's weekend with her.

"She's helping Elliott with costumes," he said. "Gemma will be picking her up soon."

"At my house?" I asked. That was just plain weird.

"Maybe," he said. "Is that okay?"

I held back the *Not at all* I wanted to say. "It's fine." My voice sounded strained.

He didn't pursue it. "The news is saying someone died."

I nodded and told him what happened. After a few attempts at explaining what we were doing there, I had to start over at the beginning of the story when I picked up Steven at Benson's house.

"You did the right thing," he said, his voice sounding offended that Yollie gave me a hard time for interfering.

I paused. "I'm not sure now. Steven's almost grown up and knows what he's doing."

He came to a stop at an intersection and glanced over at me like he wanted to argue, but one look at my bruised face must have reminded him what I'd recently gone through. "What happened after that?" he asked instead.

I told him about Yollie picking me up and heading over there, all the way through the explosion. He stopped the car hard in front of my house, with a look of disbelief on his face.

"What?" I asked.

"You smelled gas and went inside to save some guy you met once. And hated?"

"I didn't hate him," I protested. "I didn't think the concentration would be high enough..."

"To explode?"

I bit my lip and nodded. "Wouldn't most people do that?"

He gave an incredulous laugh. "No, Colbie. They wouldn't." Then he frowned, as if realizing what he was getting into by dating me and perhaps not liking it. Or maybe because that kind of thing doesn't happen to normal people.

"Well, I didn't end up saving him because he was already dead," I said.

He reached over to grab my hand. "That was too close."

I nodded, remembering Yollie's words. *It could have been worse.*

"Let me open the door for you," he said, as he came around the car.

I didn't really need the help, but I let him, since I could see how concerned he was.

I focused on not limping and ended up bumping into him when he stopped. "Are you going to look into this one?" he asked. He knew my history with murder investigations.

"No way," I said. "Norma is all over this and doesn't need any help. I'm staying away from it."

He lifted one eyebrow, clearly not believing me. Then he said, "Narrator's voice: No, she didn't."

"Not funny," I said, even though it kind of was. I turned to the front porch to see a beautiful woman watching us.

She waved. "Joss! I just saw the goats, and I swear they're already bigger." She was somehow both glamorous and athletic, wearing diamond earrings that shone through her long black hair. Sunlight caught the edge of her sunglasses, and her amazingly high cheekbones glimmered with some highlighter that I'd never be able to afford. Her cropped shirt showed rock-hard abs and her yoga pants were slung so low, they could be hip huggers.

Dismay filled my stomach. This had to Joss's ex-wife, Gemma. I mentally catalogued my explosion-blown hair, bruised face, and skinned knee. I couldn't have looked worse if I tried. I stopped my hand halfway up to smoothing my hair and put it down, knowing it was futile.

Joss stared at her, distinctly uncomfortable. He must not have thought ahead to what the two of us meeting would be like.

"Oh my goodness," she said, once she focused on me. "What happened?"

Joss guided me up the stairs, keeping himself between his ex-wife and me. "She was in an accident but she's fine."

I stopped and held out my hand. "Hi," I said, proud that my voice was clear. "I'm Colbie."

She grabbed my hand with both of hers, squeezing a little too tightly. "I'm so delighted to meet you. Kai has told me so much about you and Elliott."

"Come in," I said, working very hard to be gracious.

Just then, my dad opened the door, looking confused at the combination of people on his porch. "What are you doing chatting out here? Come in and tell me what the hell happened."

"Dad," I said, trying not to sound like my teeth were clenched. "This is Gemma, Kai's mom. Gemma, this is Hank."

He blinked at her for a moment and then said, "Welcome. Kai's a delightful kid."

"Thank you," she said. "That's so nice of you to say."

Joss seemed a bit dazed as we moved inside. Gemma stared around with interest, checking out the family photos that I'd recently put up in the hallway.

Trouble stayed on the stair landing, watching the stranger intently from between the bars.

Elliott and Kai took that moment to run out of the dining room wearing the Simba and Nala masks and singing, "I Just Can't Wait to be King."

They even did some of the choreography before starting to laugh too hard to continue.

"Oh my," Gemma said at the same time Kai noticed her.

"Hi, Mom!" Kai said. "Isn't this mask cool?"

I'd always thought that Kai looked like a miniature Joss, with his curly brown hair and blue eyes, but the high cheekbones and tiny nose were definitely her mom's.

Gemma nodded. "It certainly is. Do you have all of your stuff?"

"My backpack's in the kitchen," Kai said.

Gemma followed her for a few steps and then stopped when she saw the costume mess in the dining room.

"It gets kind of crazy around here before a show," I explained.

"Of course. What a nice little hobby for all of you," Gemma said. She turned to me. "Do you sew?"

Was that an insult? She said it in such a nice tone that I couldn't tell.

"Gemma," Joss said in a warning voice.

He knew her better than I did. I had to assume she was getting in a dig.

My dad answered her with narrowed eyes, "No, I do."

She blinked, seemingly stunned that he sewed, or maybe that he was so obviously defending me.

Then, because we needed more drama, the doorbell rang its nerve-jangling "Yankee Doodle Dandy" song, and Annie and Lani walked in.

Annie was my dad's neighbor and girlfriend. She was the one who had convinced me to move home when my dad was sick, and was now a big part of our family. She wore a sparkly hat with girl power stenciled on it and carried a plateful of baked goods. As soon as she moved closer, I caught the delicious scent of bananas and nuts.

"Hi everyone," Annie said. "I come bearing muffins. Look who I found on the porch. Lani!" Annie said as she introduced herself to Gemma.

"I'm Gemma, Kai's mother."

Joss was looking more stressed every minute. "Kai!" he called out. "Time to go."

Lani slipped by me and reached out to shake Gemma's hand. "I'm Lani." She turned to me and gave me a hug. "I come empty-handed, but full of love."

"Love for those muffins," I teased. "You can come in anyway."

"What's going on?" she whispered in my ear. Today she wore a tank top with swirls in all colors of the rainbow over purple jeans and sandals that looked like they were sprouting sunflowers from between her toes.

"Later," I said with a tight smile.

"Now, Kai!" Joss said, with a hint of desperation that I totally understood.

Finally, Kai and Elliott came out of the kitchen and their faces grew wary, sensing the tension in the room.

"Okay, then," Joss said. "Out the door." He practically shoved both his daughter and ex-wife through it.

Kai threw out a quick, "Thank you for everything," before Joss went outside and closed the door emphatically behind them.

I huffed out a deep breath. "Wow."

"Wow is right," Lani said.

"She seems like a very nice lady," Annie said, but I wasn't sure she meant it.

My dad put that all aside and grabbed me by my shoulders and looked into my face. "You're okay?" he asked as if he was demanding that I actually be okay.

"I'm good," I said.

He took a moment to pull me close for a hug and then said, "Muffins first or shower?"

"Muffins," I said. "Definitely muffins."

With the crowd thinned out a bit, Trouble came down to sniff at me. *You stink.* But she joined me when I plopped down on the couch at Annie's urging.

I filled them in on what had happened at Benson's, and none of them were surprised that I'd found another dead body. That would concern me if I wasn't so tired.

Elliott made me tell the story twice, and asked a lot of questions about how being in an explosion felt. Then he wrote down everything I said. He'd recently heard that one of his favorite writers recommended taking lots of notes about details in your life so that he could pull from them later. He was writing a play but still thought he'd be a Broadway actor when he grew up. Sometimes he said he'd be a small business owner like me, but that he'd sell something cool like skateboards instead of cat food.

I asked Lani to call Quincy and tell him that Norma would be contacting him and why. She readily agreed with my *most likely interfering with a police investigation* idea and dialed his number, but he didn't answer. She left a message for him to contact her.

My dad's concerned frown never left his face. "I don't know how you get into so much trouble."

"Like anyone could anticipate a garage exploding?" I asked.

He shook his head. "Not that. The whole dead guy thing."

I couldn't blame him, since I had gotten involved in local murder investigations before. "This one has nothing to do with me," I told him.

Trouble meowed. *That's what you said the last time.*

"So we're not going to talk about the elephant in the room?" Lani asked when my dad and Annie went into the kitchen for muffin reinforcements and probably some private smooching.

"Elephant?" I asked. "Oh you mean Joss's ex-wife." My casual tone didn't faze her.

"Yeah," she said. "She's gorgeous. And she just arranged to meet her competition."

"She did not arrange anything," I said. "She couldn't know that Joss would have to pick me up at the freakin' police station." Then I thought more about what she said. "You think she's trying to get back together with Joss?"

"I don't think it," she said. "I know it. She didn't dress like that to pick up her kid. You better watch out for her."

Great. Something else to worry about.

"Is there something wrong with me that I'm more shaken up by meeting my boyfriend's ex-wife than...you know?" I asked Lani.

"Than finding a dead body and getting blown up? Absolutely not," she said, loyal to the end. "Besides, I'm sure it's all just compounded together. Jealousy on top of extreme panic."

"Let's go with that," I said.

Chapter 4

Watching the evening news was a bad idea; reporters had driven the twenty miles inland from downtown San Diego to make wild speculations about the murder of a "beloved music teacher" in the small town of Sunnyside. At least the police hadn't released Yollie's or my name.

I slept badly and somehow turned off my alarm without gaining consciousness. My dad knocked on my door at eight, holding a cup of coffee. "You okay to go to work?" he asked. "Elliott said to let you sleep. He got a ride to school with a friend."

Trouble trailed behind him, complain-meowing loudly. *You better be okay enough to feed me.*

I sat up, trying to shake the sleep out of my brain. "What friend?" I took a sip of coffee.

"That girl who's co-vice president with him," he said, with a smile.

I smiled back. We both thought Elliott had a crush on Sasha, the girl who had battled him for the position of vice president of the drama club. At some point, they decided to be co-vice presidents and with their mutual love of musical theater, had become friends. She'd been over several times ostensibly "helping" with costumes, always right beside Elliott.

She was adorable, with dark curly hair, brown skin and brown eyes that seemed to light up when she was looking at Elliott. I think she was one of the reasons he gave in on his initial wish to have the club perform *Hairspray.* Along with Lani's costumes and the drama club teacher explaining that *The Lion King* was an epic tale of resistance against tyranny.

I'd made the mistake of asking him once if he "*liked* her liked her" and his furious denial answered me. Dad and I had met eyes and let it go.

I fed the cat and grabbed a shower, hiding the worst of the bruise on my cheek with makeup before heading out much later than normal. I arrived at my commercial kitchen to find the parking lot cordoned off with yellow police tape, the crime scene investigation truck outside. All of the employees who normally worked the early shift were milling about on the sidewalk, under the careful eye of a lone policeman behind the tape. I was already feeling anxious because both Lani and Zoey had told me they tried to call Quincy a bunch of times and he never answered or called them back. That was very unlike him.

Zoey grabbed my arm, making me wince. She was the strongest tiny person I knew. "Sorry," she said. "But you have to help Quincy."

"Start at the beginning," I said. "What's this all about?"

"Your cop friend showed up at seven a.m. with a freakin' warrant to search the entire kitchen," she said, outraged. "She said they're looking for the murder weapon and anything that could link Quincy to the murder of Benson what's-his-face."

My stomach felt like butterflies were having a death match in it. "Oh no," I said. "That's crazy."

"Tell that to your friend," Zoey said. "She looks serious as hell."

"I can't get in there and talk to her now." I bitterly resented that the two-story building had only a few windows and I had no idea what was going on inside.

"With all of those people in there, we're going to have to clean the crap out of that place before we can cook again," Zoey said. "You *have* to look into this thing."

I shook my head. "Quincy can afford the best investigator money can buy."

"Then he should hire you." She pointed at me. Zoey hated any injustice, and this kind of problem for her friend would be at the top of her list.

I should feel flattered that she believed in me so much, but I was sure Quincy would hire a professional private investigator, maybe someone who used to work for the FBI or something, especially since his life might hang in the balance.

Norma came out, followed by crime scene techs holding plastic evidence bags of kitchen tools—when I looked closer I realized they had grabbed anything that resembled a sharp stick and might be the murder weapon.

Like anyone with half a brain would actually bring something like that to work the day after a murder.

Norma was in total professional mode, brushing by me without an acknowledgement that we were friends. Her partner Detective Ragnor gave me a sympathetic smile, but I didn't know if it was because of Norma's behavior or because my friend was in trouble.

I wanted to say something in defense of Quincy, but what good would it do? Norma had to follow this path of investigation until it was finished even if it didn't lead anywhere.

We waited another hour for the last investigator to leave, grateful that they took down the crime scene tape on their way out. Zoey and I raced inside and up the metal steps to Quincy's office, our feet sounding like thunder, while the others headed into the kitchen to put it back together. Zoey beat me by a mile, and even with all of my recent running, I was huffing and puffing when I got up there.

Quincy leaned back in his desk chair, his hands folded over his stomach. He looked thoughtful rather than alarmed.

"Are you okay?" I asked.

He nodded. "I didn't do it, so they won't find anything."

"Why are they going after you so hard?" I asked. "And where were you yesterday?"

"That's the problem in a nutshell," he said "My wife got real upset about my little fight. After I talked to you, she made me go to an all-day yoga retreat in Julian. No cell phones. No electronics. I got home after dark to the press waiting outside my house with no idea why."

"Oh good," I said. "Then you have an airtight alibi."

He nodded. "I do, but according to the detective, they can't find the yogi. He took off to India or something and he doesn't own a cell phone, so until he comes back, I just might be under suspicion."

Quincy's eyebrows were furrowed. I recognized that look. He was deep in thought, exploring all of the possible ways this situation could go. When he was making a business decision, I let him have the time to think and he always came back with the most insightful statements, all the possibilities weighed against his vast experience, and then he'd say something brilliant.

This time, I didn't have the patience to wait. "What are you thinking?"

He spared us a brief glance and said, "I'm wondering why there's such an immediate big push like this. It seems to be more than me being a suspect."

"Norma's been off track before," I said. "But eventually she gets to the right person."

"Did they say why they questioned you?" Zoey pointed down to the kitchen. "And did all that?"

"Because I punched the victim," he said. "Apparently, there's a YouTube video of me threatening to 'end him' after I knocked him down." That seemed to bewilder him. "I was so angry that I don't even remember saying that."

"That can't be all they have," I said.

"Plus some texts that I sent my daughter," he said.

"How did they get those so fast?" I asked. "Never mind. What did you say?"

"Something stupid," he said, not wanting to tell us.

"How stupid?" I demanded.

"That I'd 'take care of him,'" he admitted. "Like I said, stupid."

Zoey shook her head. "Even I know better than that."

"It seems like I'm at the top of their potential suspect list." Quincy pushed a stack of legal papers toward me. "They're executing search warrants for my home and all of my businesses."

"Well, that'll keep them busy for a while," I joked. Quincy had part ownership of more companies than I could count.

"They were especially interested in Turner Furnace Repair," he said.

Uh-oh. "Do you know a lot about furnaces?"

"No," he said. "I just helped the owner get a loan last year. Why?"

"I'm pretty sure that's what blew up in the garage," I said.

He nodded. "That seems to be where Norma's questions were heading. Someone created the explosion to cover up the murder."

Zoey scowled at me. "I'm sure Colbie will do everything she can to help you."

"No. She. Won't." Quincy took off his reading glasses and pointed them at me. "I'm innocent and I don't need anyone looking into this. We all know that Norma won't rest until she gets her bad guy."

He smiled but it didn't reach his eyes. He was definitely worried.

* * * *

Commercial kitchens have strict cleaning codes, so Zoey and I helped clean every inch of the kitchen with the rest of the chefs. When we were finished, we went over the schedule to figure out how to fit in all of the cooking to fill the orders. Top priority was my monthly order for Twomey's Health Food Stores. It had only been a few months since they started selling my food and I still got a thrill when I saw it on their shelves. I'd been able to expand to keep up with the increased demand, and expected another jump in their next quarterly order.

I opened my laptop, hoping for a response from Natural-LA Grocers, but was disappointed. Now was certainly not the time to ask Quincy if he'd heard from them.

I called my friend Tod to let him know I wouldn't be able to make our normal late lunch.

"That's fine," he said, a little relief in his voice. Tod was agoraphobic and when I first met him, he hadn't been outside for years. Now he was working with a therapist who made house calls. He was making progress—allowing me to come into his apartment once a week even though it caused him some amount of anxiety, and going out for quick meals at quiet restaurants in his neighborhood. I still hoped for the Hollywood ending, where he would be completely cured and take off to some exotic location that he'd only seen online. But that wasn't happening anytime soon.

While I worked with Zoey, stir-frying chicken in a frying pan the size of a hula hoop, I couldn't help but wonder why someone killed Benson and tried to cover it up with a gas explosion. That was pretty sophisticated stuff directed at a simple oboe teacher. Not that I was going to investigate or anything. Quincy had been quite adamant.

If I *was* going to look into it, the first people I'd talk to would be his students and their parents. Steven might have been okay with his teaching methods but maybe others weren't.

The timer chimed, and I turned off the gas. I'd better focus on my food or I'd have a bunch of unhappy cat customers.

* * * *

Since Elliott had rehearsal, I stayed late at the kitchen to finish the day's production. Zoey left around three to pick up her son, and the late afternoon gang good-naturedly gave me a hard time for using some of their space. I texted my dad that I'd bring home Pico's food and he sent back a thumbs up emoji.

Yollie called me when I was on my way home, the tangy scent of the chicken burritos filling the car. "You have to help Steven."

"What's wrong?" I asked.

"Your friend the cop just questioned him about his relationship with Benson." She sounded angry. At me.

Holy cow. "I'm sure it's just standard procedure," I said. "She's probably talking to all of Benson's students."

"That's what I thought," she said. "But I called some and you know what? None of them have been questioned."

Shoot. "I'm sure she'll talk to them soon enough."

"It's your fault he's at the front of the line," she said. "You have to get him cleared."

I relented. "I'll see what Norma has to say tomorrow."

"You better," she said. "You owe him."

Oh man. Was I really going to get involved in another murder?

* * * *

By Tuesday, the news that business tycoon and philanthropist Quincy Powell was under suspicion of murder was all over the place. The YouTube video of him hitting Benson was playing on all major news stations and reporters were staked out by his house again. He texted that he was working from home, and he added, *Don't worry. It'll be fine.*

I called Norma. "Want a coffee?"

"Sure," Norma said, her voice a little too friendly.

That couldn't be good. Norma usually tried to avoid me during a murder investigation when I knew anyone involved.

Both of us knew that "coffee" meant Philz Coffee, the best in Sunnyside. By the time Norma arrived, shaking out her umbrella and shedding her raincoat, I had already ordered and paid for our large cups of my new favorite, Tantalizing Turkish, with its hint of cardamom and the addition of a fresh mint leaf, and had grabbed a corner table. It had been raining on and off for a couple of hours and clouds hung heavy in the sky.

Norma crossed the store with long strides, all business in her beige jacket thrown over her jeans. She sat down and stretched out her legs in front of her. Her eyes were tired. "Thanks," she said, reaching for the coffee.

"Good morning," I said, waiting for her to take a sip before asking her any questions.

She spoke first, getting right down to business. "Your friend has a problem."

"Which friend?" I asked, not wanting to implicate anyone.

"Quincy," she said as if it was obvious.

"Oh," I said cautiously. Norma never did this. It must be serious. "Can you tell me why?"

"Besides that fact that he has plenty of motive?" She leaned toward me and spoke quietly. "The district attorney hates Quincy and is gunning for him."

"Why?" I was stunned. Everyone loved Quincy.

"It seems Quincy had some kind of huge fundraiser for his opponent in the last election." She kept her eyes on me while she took another sip.

"Wow. Well, it looks like he won anyway," I said. "What's his problem?"

"He's the kind to hold a grudge," Norma said in a tone that showed she did not approve.

"You know Quincy, Norma," I said. "It's totally impossible for him to kill someone, especially in this way. And then trying to cover it up with arson? It's so cold-blooded. No way could he do that."

She sat back and I could almost see her brain churning. "How well do you know Yollie?"

"Really?" I may have overdone the sarcasm. "You can't possibly think she could do it. Or her son either!" I said, just as she was about to ask another question. "Creating an explosion like that takes a lot of knowledge a soccer mom just doesn't have."

She subsided.

"Aren't there, like, traffic cams or something to show you who was in the area then?" I asked.

She frowned, not liking me telling her how to do her job, but answered, "We checked the nearest traffic cam footage and saw nothing out of the ordinary."

"So you didn't see Quincy," I reinforced.

"No," she said. "But the DA pointed out that there are paths to the victim's house that avoid traffic cameras."

I sighed. "Is this guy an idiot, or does he really believe that after fighting with Benson, Quincy figured out how to sneak his way to Benson's house, avoiding all cameras, kill Benson, arrange an explosion to hide the evidence, and then sneak away—all in like twelve hours? Just because Benson said nasty things about his granddaughter?"

Norma moved as if to stand up. "We do have to 'exhaust every investigative avenue,' as he says." She used finger quotes so I knew she felt the same way I did.

"He must be a great legal mind," I said with heavy sarcasm. "I guess that's why Quincy gave money to his opponent."

A smile flitted across Norma's face.

"I thought of something last night," I said, not wanting her to leave yet. "Yollie and I must have just missed seeing the killer. Did we drive by him?"

"The garage has a door that leads to the backyard," she said. "That's most likely how he, or she, escaped without being seen."

"But the backyard has that huge hedge," I said.

"There's a way through it," she said. "It looks solid from the street, but it has a cutout to let people through to a gate."

"Quincy can't be the only one you're looking at, right? The guy was such a jerk that he had to have other people who didn't like him."

"Don't worry, we're on it," she said.

"Wait, one more thing," I said, realizing how unlikely it was that Norma would share information. "Why did you tell me about the DA? Do you *want* me to see where this goes?"

"No, not at all," she said, her voice firm.

"Because you're always telling me that amateurs shouldn't be anywhere close to murder investigations." That had never stopped her from using what I uncovered on my own though.

"And I stand by that," she said. "Of course I don't want you to get involved." She looked around to make sure no one could hear. "As long as all of the police resources are tied up with the DA's little grudge match, I won't be able to go after the real killer."

"And Quincy will be under suspicion," I said.

"Do you have anything else for me?" she asked, taking another sip. "If not, I have a search of another one of Quincy's companies to oversee."

"You know, those searches are very disruptive," I said. "Isn't that harassment or something?"

She stood up with a grim expression. "Better that than being arrested for murder."

Chapter 5

As soon as I got back to my car, I called Quincy. "A little bird told me that the DA doesn't like you very much. Did you host a fundraiser for his opponent?"

"Is that so? Interesting," he said. "Troublesome, but still interesting. There's nothing I can do until they complete their work. I know, and you know, that I'm innocent."

"But the public doesn't know," I said. "And humans like to see powerful people fall. We need to find out who the real killer is."

"Colbie," he said. "I'm not hiring someone to look into this so that I can be accused of interfering with a police investigation. You need to stay away from this."

"I have to go," I said, hanging up before he could convince me. Besides, I was pretty sure Norma had just encouraged me to see what I could find out.

* * * *

My conversation with Norma filled me with a sense of urgency. It was time to say it out loud. I was investigating another murder. How did this keep happening to me?

I called Lani and could hear her sewing machine start up again as soon as she answered the phone. "What'd you learn?" she mumbled.

"Do you have pins in your mouth again?" Her wife, Piper, was a doctor and hated that habit.

She took a few seconds to answer, so I knew she was taking them out. "Not now. Tell me everything."

I filled her in on what Norma had said. "Let's have a meeting at my house. I'm going to call Yollie and see if she and Steven can help us figure out our first steps."

* * * *

Yollie and Steven came over after school and Lani joined us. My dad was at a movie with Annie and Elliott had rehearsal, so we had an empty house.

Trouble greeted everyone as they came in, demanding attention by winding around anyone's ankles if they didn't immediately pet her. I served coffee and tea while we settled at the kitchen table.

Lani opened up my laptop and started a spreadsheet titled *Benson Suspects*. She rubbed her hands together, acting more like a supervillain than a hero. "My favorite part. Writing down the suspects!"

Yollie's eyes widened.

"Don't worry," Lani said. "Pretty soon it'll become old hat."

"I certainly hope not," Yollie said.

Steven scowled at Lani and I realized that he probably had some complicated emotions about Benson's death.

"Steven, I'm really sorry for your loss," I said. "I know this is particularly hard for you, but the police are focused on Quincy and I need to give them other ideas about who could have done this."

"How do you know he didn't?" His tone was belligerent.

"One, because he has a solid alibi that the police will confirm. Eventually," I said. "But also because I know him very well, and he's just not capable of killing someone."

He met my eyes, and the anger in his face changed to sadness. "Can we hurry this up? I have to practice."

"Can you tell me what Norma asked you?"

He looked at his mom, who nodded.

He shrugged. "She just asked a lot of questions about what happened that morning, and what I knew about...Benson."

"What'd you say?" Lani asked.

He repeated the details about my interrupting his lesson, and what he'd heard about Quincy punching Benson. None of that was good for Quincy.

"What else do you know about Benson?"

"I don't know," he said. "He was just my teacher."

"Had he been acting any differently lately?" I asked.

"No." He pulled at a loose thread on his sleeve. "I told the detective the same thing. He was the same."

"Do you know of any students or their parents who were mad at him?"
I tried.

He pushed his hand through his hair. "Lots of them. Everyone wants
a great recommendation but not everyone gets one. All of us seniors are
trying to get into college and auditioning, and it's crazy. We're all crazy."

Lani typed in *Students* and on a separate line, *Parents*.

"Anyone in particular?" I asked.

"There was some dad on his Facebook page who said he was going to
sue him," Steven said. "Maybe start with him."

I almost laughed when I saw Lani type *Mad Dad*.

"How many students has Benson taught over the years?" I asked, hoping
it was a manageable number.

He shrugged. "Forty? Fifty? Maybe more. I don't really know."

Oh no. That was too many to investigate. "Did past students like him?"

He paused a moment to find the right words. "Look," he said. "Some
teachers are your, like, mentors for life. Benson wasn't like that. He just
wanted to teach music and help you get into college and then you were on
your own. Some people were offended."

Lani typed *Past Students* as a separate category on the spreadsheet.
"What did he do when he wasn't teaching? Did he play in a jazz group
or something?"

"Yes," Steven said. "He did lots of freelance work. Substituting for the
local symphony, and like, lots of recording gigs. He had his own woodwind
quintet too, and he always invited us students to those performances."

"There are lots of motives for murder," Lani said, as if she was an
expert. "Jealousy, money, revenge, love. Did Benson ever talk about dating
or anything personal?"

"No," he said, but seemed uncomfortable. We all could tell that he
knew something.

"Spill it," Yollie said in her mom voice.

"Geez," he said and then added as if it was painful to say. "I saw someone
leave on Saturday morning a few weeks ago."

"Ooh," Lani said. "The walk of shame."

Steven cringed.

"Did you recognize her?" I asked.

"Or him?" Lani added with a frown at me for assuming. She typed in
Lovers.

Steven nodded. "It was the secretary at my school. Ms. Volker."

"Opal Volker?" Yollie asked, sounding a bit horrified. "The counseling
secretary?"

"Yeah," he said. He may have shuddered.

Yollie turned to me. "The parents hate her. She's awful to just about everyone."

"Then why is she still there?" I asked.

"No one knows," she said.

"How can I talk to her?" I asked.

She scowled. "She never responds to voice messages. Ever. Some parents just show up at her office."

"Looks like you're going to high school," Lani said to me a little too gleefully.

"Great," I said. "My least favorite part of my life."

"Ooh," Lani added, staring at the computer. "Mad Dad is actually Fred Hugo and boy did he go off on Benson. Also, according to his very public Facebook page, he 'likes' the Sunnyside Library Family Movie Nights." She smiled at me. "Looks like you're also going to the movies."

"Whoever killed Benson had to know that he was alone on Sunday mornings," Yollie said. "And that's a lot of people. His students and their parents all knew he spent most of every Sunday practicing or making reeds. Maybe a lot of other people knew that too."

"Reeds?" I asked.

Steven nodded. "Every serious oboist makes their own reeds."

"Can't you buy them?"

He blew out a breath as if the idea was ridiculous. "Those are awful. If you want to sound good, you have to master making your own reeds. They take a long time to make and even if you get a perfect one, lots of things can go wrong."

Yollie explained. "You have to scrape bamboo to be the perfect size and the perfect width. Like to one micrometer." She squeezed two fingers together. "All oboists spend hours a day, on top of practicing, scraping away at reeds."

"Do you have to do that with other instruments?" I asked.

"No," he said, a little wary as if he knew what I was going to ask next.

"Then why did you choose to play the oboe?"

He jutted out his jaw like he'd heard that question a million times. "*Because* it is so difficult," he said. "It's both mentally and physically challenging like no other instrument in the world."

Yollie explained. "Exceptional musicians have to be obsessive, but oboists take it the next level. They're their own breed of musician."

"Mom," he said, embarrassed.

"I think that's cool." I remembered the tools I'd seen when I barged into his lesson. "Hey, does, did, Benson use the tools he had in the garage?"

Steven nodded. "Yeah. He had tools to hold the bamboo in place and razors to scrape them."

"Could one of them be used to, like, poke someone?"

Steven eyes widened. "A mandrel."

"What's that?" I asked.

Lani typed away on her computer and then turned it around to show the images of various sizes of a small tool that looked like a stick.

"It's what you put the reed on to help hold it in place," he explained.

Lani turned the computer back, both of us thinking the same thing. Someone had used Benson's own tool to kill him. "You know, you should get Tod to look into this."

"Tod?" Steven asked.

"He's a friend who knows how to use the internet to find out information," I explained.

"A hacker?" he asked.

"No," I said. "Definitely not a hacker."

"Oh." He seemed disappointed.

"But he knows hackers," I said.

"Oh my God," Yollie said, staring at her phone.

"What?" we all asked together.

She grabbed Steven's arm. "Tabitha Higgins is taking auditions. She's opening up her schedule to make room for a few of Benson's students!"

"Is that okay?" I asked. "It sounds like she's taking advantage."

Yollie looked shocked. "Tabitha is the best oboe teacher in all of Southern California. She has been closed to new students for years. Steven couldn't even get an audition before."

"Sign me up, Mom," Steven said. "Hurry."

She clicked on her phone. "You have an audition Thursday morning. I'll get you out of school." She turned back to me. "She's being extremely gracious—she's very busy and doesn't need to squeeze in more students."

Lani had gone back to typing away on the computer, and I'd bet I was going to find a bunch of information about mandrels when I got it back from her.

"Maybe we should talk to this Tabitha about Benson," I suggested.

Yollie's mouth opened and closed like a fish for a moment. "Don't. You. Dare. She doesn't have anything to do with his...death."

"Of course not," I said. "But maybe she'd have ideas of who might hate him enough to, you know."

"Not until after Steven's audition." She pointed her finger at me. "You messed up with Benson. I'm not letting you do that with Tabitha."

"Mom," Steven said, embarrassed by his mom again.

"Yollie," I said, keeping my voice calm like I did when Elliott was too emotional to make a good decision. "Someone murdered Benson. Tabitha might know something that will clear Quincy. It might not seem like it, but finding out who did it is more important than Steven getting into the right college."

She scowled stubbornly. "You know, when Elliott is applying to college, I'm going to remind you of this conversation."

"Okay," I relented. "After his audition."

"And don't mention Steven's or my name at all."

"Deal."

I took her grudging scowl for a metaphorical handshake.

"Okay," I said. "We have the beginning of a plan. I'm going to speak to this Opal Volker and Steven is going to ask around to find out if any students or parents were mad at Benson." I usually had more to work with, but I looked at the clock. We were out of time. "Sorry, you guys have to go."

"So you can go on your hot date," Lani added, making Steven grimace. Yollie hit his arm as they stood up. "Stop it. Moms are allowed to date."

"I know," Steven said, "But can you please not talk about it?" His tone made it seem like the whole idea was painful for him.

After they left, I took a minute to look at what Lani had pulled up, trying to figure out if that tool could have been the murder weapon based on the quick glimpse I'd seen of Benson's wound.

I wasn't going to be able to figure it out with Google images, so I cleaned up and headed over to the farm. Joss had made lasagna and salad, and we sat on his front porch to eat as the sun set. After dinner, we held hands as we walked over to the goat pen and watched them settle in for the night. They curled up around each other, their hooves tucked under their chests.

I decided to get the tough stuff out of the way. "So I finally met Gemma."

He looked at me warily. "Yeah."

I decided to go for it. "You never said how beautiful she was." I was very proud of my casual tone.

"Right, 'cause that's something you mention to your new girlfriend," he said.

I was immediately stuck on the word "girlfriend." We'd been very careful to say "dating," and hadn't defined it any more than that. I felt a rush of warmth.

"I'm sorry she said that about, you know," he said.

"Our little hobby?" I quoted, smiling.

He looked chagrined. "I apologize for her," he said. "I have a feeling I'm going to be apologizing for her a lot more. She's got strong opinions about how Kai should be spending her time."

"Oh." I did not want to get involved in any parenting conflicts. Besides, it was only fair that I met Gemma. Joss had become used to Richard's visits with Elliott and had easily accepted that Elliott's dad would be around. I should be just as gracious.

"My dad's been asking about Thanksgiving," I said. "He'd love a big get-together. Any chance you and Kai can come?"

He blinked, making me wonder if he thought I was getting more serious than he was.

I rushed on. "Annie will be there, and Lani and Piper, if she's not on duty, and maybe even Tod. Although he probably won't be able to come." I hadn't thought of Tod before—it was just to show that inviting Joss wasn't that big of a deal—but I liked the idea as soon as I said it.

He grabbed my hand. "I'd love to," he said. "I get Kai for Thanksgiving and Gemma gets her for Christmas Day, so it would be wonderful to join your family at your house."

I smiled. "Great. It's settled then."

"So when is Elliott getting home?" He pulled me close, running his hands up my back.

"We've got time," I said.

Chapter 6

I woke up the next morning to Quincy's full-on public relations response to reporters. My social media notifications were through the roof, and business owners who had worked with Quincy over the years were all over the news, making statements in support of him.

I breathed a sigh of relief, even though I knew Quincy wasn't out of the woods yet. But at least he was fighting back.

At breakfast, which included pancakes in the shape of elephants, I gave my dad the good news about Joss and Kai coming for Thanksgiving and he was delighted. My dad's family was far away in Boston and we spent my early years going to our friends' houses for holiday dinners. Now that Elliott and I were living with him, he was trying to create a new family tradition and including all of our friends was part of it.

Joss had moved to Sunnyside from Alaska to follow his daughter when Gemma moved closer to her family. Now, he only went home during the summer when weather was less likely to interfere with his travel.

I had my own issues with my ex. I'd dropped out of college during my freshman year when I got pregnant. Elliott's father, Richard Winston III, had been yanked back home to New York by his family. For twelve years, he wanted nothing to do with his son. And then a couple of months ago, he appeared on our doorstep.

Elliott and his "bio-dad," as I still called him when he wasn't around, were working on their relationship and I tried to stay out of it as much as possible. Richard visited whenever he was on the West Coast. Since his extended family had businesses and homes in San Francisco, he was here enough that he had a regular room in the local bed-and-breakfast, where he had reportedly charmed the owner so much, that she started calling his room, Richard's Room.

In October, he'd flown Elliott to New York over a long weekend. It was the furthest Elliott had ever been from me and I had felt it like a sharp pain in my chest. Richard took Elliott to see *Hamilton* on Broadway and even got him backstage. I guess having tons of money provides all kinds of opportunities Elliott didn't get with me.

I worried the whole time he was gone, no matter what my dad and Lani said. Along with all the normal *visiting the big bad city* worries, was the awful thought that Elliott would prefer the rich lifestyle that Richard could give him.

But that hadn't happened. Elliott had been terribly homesick, had not enjoyed meeting Richard's wife at all, and couldn't wait to get back to Sunnyside. Richard had hinted at picking up Elliott the day after Thanksgiving to go to San Francisco, but I was ignoring that until I was asked directly.

* * * *

Zoey was late. That had never happened since I hired her to be my head chef. Not seeing her at the kitchen threw me for a loop. She was never not there when she was supposed to be.

I called her and she answered. "Are you okay?" I asked.

"Sorry," she said. "I'm... sick." She certainly sounded funny.

"No problem," I said. "I'll handle the cooking today."

"Thanks," she said, sounding distracted. She hung up without any further explanation.

She must be really sick.

Uri, one of the bakers who worked at the next counter, came in and said, "Hey. Did you see that supreme muscle car in the parking lot?"

"Nope, missed it," I said. I rarely paid attention to cars.

Then a thought wriggled into my brain and wouldn't go away. It wouldn't have even come into my mind on a normal day. But Zoey wasn't here and she sounded weird. She'd once told me her ex-boyfriend drove a muscle car—the same language as Uri had used. She'd also said that he was violent and she hoped he stayed out of her and her son Zeke's lives forever.

The coincidence was too much.

She rarely mentioned him, but I knew he was the father of her son and that she was grateful he didn't want anything to do with them. But she also worried that he could change his mind at any time.

"What color is the car?" I asked Uri.

It sounded more like a demand and he gave me a look. "Dark green, you know, the money color."

I grabbed my phone and headed outside, turning on the camera app as I walked. I could see the car from the doorway. The front end seemed to lean forward, making me think that a panther had transformed into a sports car. A man with light red hair pulled back into a ponytail sat inside the car with the engine off and the windows open.

I was about to step out when Uri came up behind me. "What are you up to?" he asked, making me jump and let out a squawk.

"I need to get a photo," I said. "And find out why he's here."

He held up his own phone. "I can do it."

"Thanks. I need to talk to him," I said. Uri had played football in college. If this guy was actually Zoey's ex, I might need him. "Can you be my backup just in case, I don't know, something happens?"

He clicked on his camera app. "Sure."

I took a couple of photos of the license plate and continued snapping away as I came around the side of the car. Then I looked down, switched the camera app to video and started rolling. By now, the driver had to know I was there.

"Can I help you?" I asked.

He turned toward me, and I realized that if this *was* Zoey's ex, I knew why. With his high cheekbones and large eyes, he could be a runway model. He smiled. "No, you can't," he said. "So get your little butt back in there and cook."

"I'm the owner," I lied easily. "Who are you waiting for?"

He looked me up and down. "No, you ain't," he said. "And it's none of your business, little girl."

I tapped down my anger and faked a laugh. "Little girl? I'm old enough to be your mother."

"Dang," he said. "You still gotta get outta my face."

I lifted one hand. "I wish I could, but this is my parking lot. So you can tell me what you're doing here, or I'll call the cops."

He slammed both hands on the steering wheel with a loud, "Gah! Why you gotta get in my business? Why you gotta be such a bitch?"

I took a few steps back, his escalating anger making me nervous. Uri started walking toward me, and I took a deep breath.

"Fine," I said. "Have it your way." I turned around and dialed 911. Then I heard the car door open and whirled around. He got out of the car, but he didn't come after me. He slammed the door closed so hard that it rocked the vehicle. Then he started kicking his own car.

I'd never seen anyone lose their temper so quickly and so completely. Uri stopped beside me, his phone in front of his face, recording the whole thing. "He's out of his freakin' mind."

The driver stopped suddenly, looking at the damage he'd caused to his own car. Then he threw his hands in the air and yelled at me, "Look what you made me do!"

* * * *

We retreated to the doorway while he paced around his car a few times and then the police arrived, two patrol cars blocking the entrance. They approached him cautiously, and he practically shape-shifted, becoming a charming and agreeable person who didn't know why the police had been called.

I texted a photo to Zoey along with the message, *Is this him?*

She texted back. *OMG. That's Red, my ex. Are you okay?*

I'm fine, I said. *Are you??*

I don't know.

The police are here, I said. *Don't you have a restraining order against him?*

Yes, she said. *Not that it ever helped.*

The police took statements from Uri and me, and I mentioned the restraining order. Uri also supplied them with the video of Red losing his nut. That drew the most response from them, and I was grateful he'd stuck around and taken it.

Red claimed that he was just resting, that he didn't know Zoey worked here, that he'd simply been insulted that I was trying to kick him out of a public place.

Luckily, after seeing the video, the police cuffed him and put him in the back of the patrol car. He didn't complain. He just kept saying he didn't understand what the problem was.

As they drove away, he stared at me all the way out of the parking lot. He definitely thought I was the problem.

* * * *

Zoey had told me we'd talk later that night, so I focused on catching up on the day's production. It was much harder without her. In between batches, I pulled off my kitchen gloves and kept dialing Opal Volker, the counseling secretary, trying to catch her in. It was a complete waste of time. Was she ever at her desk? Did she just send *all* of her calls through to voice mail? Finally, I gave up and left a message.

Two hours later, nothing.

I really didn't want to go to Sunnyside High School.

I called Yollie. "Do you think she'll call me back?"

"I told you, it's like pulling teeth to get her to contact you," she said. "You should go there." I heard a timer chime through the phone. "Gotta go wash out a client."

I looked in the mirror at the copper stripe in my hair. It was fading fast. I made a mental note to make an appointment with her.

I resigned myself to the inevitable and drove over to the school, parking in the lot for visitors. Several signs said that I had to check in at the Administration Office, where I wrote my name and received directions and a red sticker that I assumed let me roam the school unchallenged.

I made my way to the Counseling Office, only to find a line of students waiting outside and the door locked.

"Why is it locked?" I asked the student leaning against the wall staring at her phone.

She blinked a few times before answering. "It's scheduling time for next semester."

"Okay." I still didn't understand. "Doesn't that mean the door should be unlocked?"

She snorted with derision. "They open it for a half hour at lunch and then for last period, at two thirty."

A girl behind her with blue hair spoke up. "Your kid must be new here. The counseling staff turns into raving lunatics right after the schedules are sent out. It's to keep us from complaining too much about what they signed us up for."

"That doesn't make any sense," I said. "Aren't they here to help you?"

"Welcome to high school," Blue Haired Girl said. She looked at her watch. "If I don't get into AP Bio, I'm screwed."

I joined the line and waited to see the process. A woman opened the door at two thirty, and not one minute before. She was about my age, with curly brown hair pulled back with a headband. She scowled at the line and propped the door open. "Sign in."

Walking behind the counter, she stood in the hallway leading to the offices of the school counselors, her stance wide like a bouncer. "Incoming!" she yelled.

One of the counselors came out of her office. "Thank you Opal," she said, sounding annoyed. I wasn't sure if it was directed at Opal or the students, but she called the first name on the list. Two other counselors stepped out and called the next students, all carefully crossing off the name they'd called.

Once the students moved by, I walked to the counter. Before I could even ask a question, Opal bellowed, "Sign in!"

"But I was hoping to talk to you, not the counselors," I said.

She looked confused. "Why?"

"Um." I looked around. "It's kind of personal."

She huffed and said, "This is a counseling office for students, not parents."

"No, I mean it's personal to you," I explained.

She gave me a look like she didn't believe me, but stepped closer, triangulating her position in the room so she could keep an eye on the path to the offices. "What is it?"

"I heard that you dated Benson Tadworth," I said in a low tone.

Her face froze and she hissed, "Not. Here."

"It's the only way I could think of to get in touch with you," I said.

"What do you want?"

"I'm just trying to figure out why someone would do something like that," I asked. "Do you have any ideas?"

"No," she said. "Get out now."

When I tried to protest, she repeated in an *Exorcist* voice, "Now."

A couple of the students were looking at me over their phones, so I decided to retreat. "Here's my card," I said and held it out to her.

She just glared at me and I left it on the counter.

Chapter 7

I was on my way home from the unsuccessful trip when I got a call from my dad. "There's a woman here."

"Okay," I said slowly, wondering what the problem could be.

"She said she's inspecting the puppets." He seemed agitated.

"Oh sorry," I said. "I meant to tell you about her. But I thought she was coming tomorrow."

"She's in the dining room," he said. "She has purple hair!"

"From what I know, puppeteers are about the nicest people on the planet," I said. "I'll be there soon."

Lani had told me that the local puppetry guild members were very dedicated to teaching the students how to properly control their puppets. They were insistent that the puppets be safe for both the actors and the audience, especially the ones that would be paraded through the aisles. They had a gentle way of convincing the students to fix any issues.

Lani's costume motto was that if a mistake couldn't be seen from the front row, then it was fine, but that didn't work for the guild. They'd fixed some of the puppets and helped make them into works of art.

My dad must have heard me drive up because he opened the front door for me, looking a little upset. "She closed the door."

"Dad, she's a puppeteer, not a serial killer," I said, but I humored him and went directly to meet her. "Hi, I'm Colbie."

"Hello. I'm Tuesday." A middle-aged woman with pink and purple streaks in her hair placed a papier-mâché head of a hyena over her head, then turned back and forth, and tilted it in all directions, as if testing how an actor would move in it. She took off the head and made some notes on a clipboard.

"What an unusual name," I said. "Can I help you with anything?"

"No," she said. "I got it." She picked up a shirt of a hyena costume and put it on as well. It had gloves attached that looked like giant hyena paws. She hummed happily while gesturing wildly with the paws. "Good," she said, and took it off to make more notes.

"My son is so happy with his Zazu puppet," I said. "He's been practicing all over the house."

She smiled. "He's doing such a nice job. He's a natural at puppetry."

Just what any mother wants to hear. "Thank you." *I think.*

When she moved on to an antelope puppet and frowned at a dent in the nose, I decided I wasn't needed. I couldn't imagine this nice lady absconding with the family silver. Not that there was any. "Let me know if you need anything."

"I will." She turned the antelope head toward me and expertly made its mouth move to her words. "Thanks for letting me check out the puppets before we move everything to the school for dress rehearsal."

I had a hard time looking at her and not the puppet, and I had to smile. "You're welcome." I couldn't believe it, but I might actually miss all of the creative mess in my dining room.

"Your group is so lucky," she said.

"We are?"

"Hmm." She checked out the bottom of a cheetah mask. "The anonymous donation helped so much."

"Donation?"

She pursed her lips, as if wondering how I didn't know about it. "Someone made an anonymous donation for the puppets—the rentals, the materials, the building, and our training time."

"Oh right," I said. "I didn't realize it was that significant."

She smiled brilliantly. "Oh it was. It made our work so much easier. Your group has a guardian angel."

I had a hunch I knew who the "guardian angel" was, but I wasn't sure what to do about it.

* * * *

Pico's was my family's favorite restaurant, and had become our home away from home. The owner was relentlessly friendly, winning the hearts of all of his customers, from the businessmen who jammed in at his counter for a quick lunch, to the families who sat around the linoleum tables for hours.

Only new customers noticed the odd décor. Pico had bought a diner and slapped a cheap Pico's Restaurant sign over the diner sign. He ran the restaurant with his family, serving traditional Mexican food in a super casual, welcoming environment.

He gave me a big hug when I arrived, towering over me and smelling like tomatoes, onions and spice. "I saved your favorite table for you and your girls," he said. Lani, Norma, and I had set aside Wednesday evenings for Margarita Night, and we all tried hard to make it regularly, every week we could.

Lani and I liked to say that Norma was the flakiest of the group, despite being the least flaky person I'd ever met. She got called away to work at the last minute quite often, so we never knew if we were going to see her until she showed up.

She shared custody of her daughter with her ex-husband who was also a cop, and he sometimes had to bail on his night with his daughter. Not that she ever talked about him, or her current dating life, no matter how much we dished about ourselves and hinted to her that it was her turn.

Perhaps it was the way we met—when she suspected me of murder— which dictated we'd never be the kind of BFFs who shared stuff like dating or our deepest darkest secrets.

That wasn't going to stop me from asking questions about her investigation into my friend.

Pico delivered our margaritas, frowning. He had started blending fresh mangoes in and I loved the sweetness playing against the tangy citrus of his own special blend. The tequila that he imported specially from Mexico helped too.

"Yo," he said. "You see that guy at the counter?"

I moved my head and could see only a group of men who had taken off their suit jackets and rolled up their sleeves. "Who?"

He looked over his shoulder. "Shoot. He ain't there."

"What's wrong?" I asked.

"He was asking about you," he said, straining to look out the window to see where the man had gone. "Asking if you come here a lot."

"Ooh," Lani said. "Joss has some competition."

I rolled my eyes at her. "What did he look like?"

"I didn't get a good look," he said. "My son talked to him." He gave an exasperated sniff. "Let me get him." He expertly made his way through the tables in spite of his bulk, and we watched him having an arm-waving conversation with his son who was half his size.

"I don't understand what the fuss is," Lani said.

"Me neither." I turned back to her. "I got nothing out of Opal Volker," I started, but then Pico appeared beside me.

"I apologize in advance for my son's lack of paying attention to important details like what the guy freakin' looked like." Pico yelled the last few words toward his son, who waved his towel at him in disgust.

"What's the big deal?" I asked.

"It's just plain weird," he said. "My idiot son said the guy gave him the creeps but he doesn't even remember what he looks like. Just average, like, everything."

Pico's agitation was contagious and I tried to look out the window, but the way the light from the setting sun hit the glass made it impossible. "Well, let me know if he comes back," I said.

Then Norma came in and Pico left to get her margarita and to refill the chips. She held up two hands in an *I surrender* position, "No questions until I eat," she said.

Lani rubbed her hands together. "Let's get her liquored up and interrogate her."

Norma looked tired but I knew better than to say anything about it. Instead, I talked about Joss's goats and Elliott deciding to narrate my dad's football game using his Zazu voice and puppet.

I told them about my conversation with Tuesday, the puppet inspector. "So now I have to talk to Richard and see if he's the so-called guardian angel of the middle school drama club."

"Why?" Lani asked. "Let him help them out."

"Someone is going to spill the beans or figure out it's Elliott's dad, and then any time he gets a good role, they'll say it's because of the money."

"Oh." Lani sipped her margarita through the straw. "Maybe you should ask Elliott how he feels about it and let him talk to Richard."

Darn. She was right. "At least she approved all of the puppets, and took half of them to the theater at the school."

Finally Norma seemed fed and relaxed enough that I could ask her a question. "So, anything you can tell us?" I held my breath, not knowing if Norma would help or not.

She gave a heavy sigh. "Why don't you go first? What have you learned so far?"

I told her about Lani's list of suspects, but didn't have much else to report.

"Steven is supposed to ask around and find out if any students or their parents were mad at Benson," Lani added. "But he's busy preparing for his audition. What can you tell us?"

"Well," she said. "The only thing I can say is that Quincy isn't our only suspect."

"Is he still your primary one?" I asked.

She frowned and didn't answer. "I wonder if you can help me with something. Steven said that the victim received a phone call on Saturday morning."

I nodded. "I saw him on the phone."

"His records don't show a call," Norma said.

"Whoa," Lani said.

"That's weird," I said. "Unless he has more than one phone."

Norma grew thoughtful. "I have to go."

Lani and I called it an early night and I texted Zoey once I got home. I started and deleted several messages before sending *I'm here if you want to talk.*

Three dots appeared, indicating that she was responding.

Then they disappeared.

* * * *

Zoey was at work the next day and I cornered her in the dry storage room. "You want to tell me what's going on?"

She sank down on a step stool, looking like she hadn't slept much.

"I'm too tired to argue with my boss," she said.

"What do you mean argue?" I said. "And right now I'm not your boss. I'm your friend, and I want to help you."

"I don't think anyone can do anything to help." She sounded like she'd lost all hope.

"Just start at the beginning," I said. "All I know is that you had an abusive boyfriend who stalked you at the restaurant you worked at before here."

"Yeah," she said. "He's Zeke's dad and he's like a freakin' anchor on my life." The last word came out loud and so distraught my throat ached for her.

"He was gone for a while," I said. "Why is he back?"

"His girlfriend kicked him out and now he's living at home with his mother. I guess that means he has the time and energy to come after me," she said.

"Why isn't he going after that girlfriend?" I asked.

"He was harassing her, and she sent some biker friends to set him straight," she said. "So now he's back to me."

Someone came in for a twenty pound bag of whole wheat flour. I waited for them to leave to ask, "What happened to make you not come in yesterday?"

She shook her head. "That—" she stopped herself from calling him a nasty name. "He went to Zeke's school. My poor kid is in kindergarten, and Red went to his school demanding to see him."

"What happened?" I asked, holding my breath.

"Thank God the secretary checked the list and saw that Red's not allowed to see him. So he caused a scene. Throwing things around the office and yelling. He refused to leave until the security guard arrived and threatened to throw him out."

"What'd you do?" I asked. "Where's Zeke today?"

"I pulled him out of school," she said. "He's at a friend's house, someone that Red doesn't know. He's staying there until Red moves on." She shook her head. "I'm afraid, Colbie," she whispered. "I hate being afraid."

"I'm so sorry," I said, feeling helpless.

"It's not your fault," she said. "It's my fault. I'm the one who got involved with him, and then had a baby with him, when I knew he had that crazy temper. Why did I do that? Now I'm chained to him through my son."

"Maybe you thought he could be better," I said. "A better man."

She nodded. "I was fooling myself. He's never going to change."

"Is there anything I can do?" I asked. "Maybe I should talk to Norma and see what she recommends."

Zoey looked defeated. "I tried the police so many times…it never works."

"Norma is different," I said. "She would take action."

"Oh yeah? Then why hasn't Quincy been cleared yet?" she demanded. "The press is still all over him."

"You know, it's only been like four days," I reminded her.

"It feels longer," she said. "You should get your hacker friend to see what he can find out."

Lani had recommended the same thing and I'd dropped the ball. "He's not a hacker."

Zoey stood up. "Let's get to work. At least that's something I can do."

We went back to the kitchen area and planned the products to finish that day. Zoey went to collect the ingredients from the freezer.

"I have to make a call," I told her and went outside to phone Tod.

"Hi Colbie," he said. "You want me to look into that Benson guy?"

"How did you know that's why I was calling you?"

"You always want me to help," he said. "I'll let you know what I dig up."

As soon as I made it back to my station in the kitchen, Yollie called. "Norma just texted me. She wants Steven to identify Benson's phone. What's that about?"

Whoa. "She must have found a second phone." I debated calling Norma to find out. "Why would he need that?"

"I have no idea," Yollie said.

"Can you let me know what Norma tells you?" I asked.

"Hold on. I'll be right there," she called out to someone, her voice muffled. "I told her not to bother Steven. His big audition with Tabitha is this morning. Norma's going to stop by tonight when we're both home."

"Ask her anything you can think of," I suggested. "And let me know everything she says."

Yollie agreed. "You can call Tabitha this afternoon," she added. "But don't use either of our names."

I rolled my eyes. "Of course not."

Zoey was watching me with interest. "What's going on?"

"Just doing what you said," I told her. "And going wherever it takes me."

Chapter 8

At exactly five minutes after noon, I emailed Tabitha Higgins, asking if she had time to meet. She responded right away, saying she had availability from three to four p.m. on Monday, or two to three p.m. on Thursday. Whoa. She was certainly tight with her schedule. I grabbed the Monday slot and she emailed back that we could meet at Honey's Bistro in Encinitas, near her home.

Okay, again, that was very specific.

Then I saw that I'd received an email from Natural-LA Grocers! My stomach fluttered and I clicked on it. All it said was they were taking my proposal under advisement and would let me know when a decision was made.

Well that was disappointing. Trying not to feel totally deflated, I called Quincy to see if he had heard anything more.

"I got the same email," he said. "I'm sorry."

"It's not your fault," I said. "They just haven't made a decision yet."

"Unfortunately, it is my fault," he said. "My contact said they put the proposal on ice until the investigation into Benson's death is over."

"What?"

"They're concerned about the bad publicity," he explained. "So, it really is my fault. If I hadn't punched that man, you might have gotten the green light by now."

"Oh for crying out loud," I said. "That's ridiculous."

"It's business, Colbie."

"Whatever. But you cannot blame yourself. I wouldn't even be in the position to make a proposal if you hadn't helped me. And if they're stupid enough to say no, we'll find another company." My voice had gotten steadily louder until everyone in the kitchen was staring at me.

Quincy laughed. "That's my girl."

* * * *

I was still fuming hours later when I arrived at the Sunnyside Farmers' Market. My outrage gave me more energy to unload my car quickly. I set up faster than ever, but was not in the right mood to deal with customers.

Trouble meowed at me from the cat carrier. *Chill*. She even swatted at me when I tried to put her chef's hat on and the elastic snapped back onto my hand.

"Okay," I said. "I'll be good."

She grumbled but settled onto her blue cat-sized love seat that matched the blue on my Meowio labels.

I rearranged the non-cat food products that always went over well at these markets—the coffee mugs with a cartoon of Trouble in a chef's hat, the kitchen utensils with paw prints running across the handles, and my newest addition, small stuffed cats in Trouble's image with a chef's hat, of course!

The Sunnyside Farmers' Market was held every Thursday afternoon in the park behind the library. It was run by the education foundation and a portion of our booth rentals went to the schools.

I forced myself to take deep breaths to prepare for the onslaught of parents and children arriving after school. Trouble was always on her best behavior. I better be too.

The time passed quickly. Lots of my local customers stopped by my booth to chat and avoid shipping costs.

One of my earliest and most consistent customers picked up a case of Seafood Romance and asked, "Hey, why is Pico's closed?"

"It's closed?" I asked. I was just there yesterday. That didn't make sense.

"I thought you would know since you go there all the time," she said.

Hmm. I was getting a reputation. Maybe I should cut back. Then I thought about Pico's chicken burritos and knew there wasn't a chance.

After she left, I called the restaurant and got a recording that Pico's would be closed for a few days. That was weird.

I dialed Pico's personal cell number. "You on vacation and didn't tell me?"

"Nah," he said. "I'm going nuts. Someone let a bunch of crickets loose in the kitchen."

"What?"

"I know, it's crazy."

"Why would someone do that?" I asked. Everyone loved Pico.

"My sons think it's another restaurant causing us problems, but that don't make no sense," he said. "I even called the cops and they think it's a frat boy prank, or something."

"That makes even less sense," I said. "Where are the frat boys going to get the best burritos in San Diego if you're not open?"

"I said the exact same thing," he said. "Hey. Maybe you can come solve that mystery for me."

I seriously considered it. "Did the police look at the tapes from the security cameras?"

"Sure did," he said. "But someone cut the freakin' wire."

"Just to leave a bunch of crickets?" I asked. "That's even stranger. How are you going to get rid of them?"

"Junior here wants to buy a bunch of lizards, but I got the exterminators coming tomorrow," he said. "I'll be back open in no time. They make the most god awful sound."

I laughed. "Guess I'll have to get pizza tonight."

"You're breaking my heart, girl," he said, but I could tell he was smiling.

After I packed up, I called Chubby's Pizza, ordering the deep dish Chicago-style pizza with sausage and pepperoni that my dad and Elliott loved. They wouldn't complain about the change in dinner plans.

I drove over to the restaurant, cracking the car window for Trouble, and waited inside by the pickup window. A man came in behind me and asked, "Waiting for your food?" He seemed to be one of those overly friendly guys who didn't mind asking the obvious.

"Yep," I said. The smell of tomato and garlic had my stomach growling.

He nodded and pulled his pants up over his beer belly. "Me too. Can't wait." He laughed, sounding a bit like a donkey, and shifted in place, like he had too much energy and didn't know what to do with it.

I smiled stiffly, not wanting to be unfriendly, but not wanting to encourage him in any way. He could easily be the type to talk someone's ear off.

"I like your shirt," he said. "Is that for cat food?"

"Yes," I said. I rarely regretted wearing the shirt advertising my business, but this was one of those times.

He looked confused. "Does your cat eat that brand or something?"

I nodded. "Yes, and it's my business. I started it because she and lots of cats have digestive issues, and eating organic food is better for them."

"Really?" he asked. "Is that a good business to be in?"

"It's doing okay," I said. I don't think I ever got that question before.

"'Cause I'm the entrepreneurial type and I might be interested in something like that."

"It's not for sale," I said, my tone a little sharp.

"And you don't like, franchise it?"

"No."

"Huh," he said, then changed gears. "My cat sometimes throws up after he eats. Do you think your food would be good for him?"

"It's worth a try," I said.

"Where can I buy it?"

"At Twomey's Health Food Stores or straight from the website." I dug a card out of my purse that had the website and business phone number on it. "And I sell it at local farmers' markets too."

"Cool," he said. "I go to the Sunnyside one all the time. You sell there?" When I nodded, he added, "I'm surprised I never saw you there."

"There are a lot of people," I said in a noncommittal tone.

"That's the truth," he said. "Here's my card. I'm Drake Frost. I just got out of the insurance business, and now I'm selling nutritional supplements." His card had the name of a well-known multilevel marketing company on it.

Ah. That explained his friendliness. He was looking for people to start selling through him to build the next layer of the pyramid. Newbies were trained to talk to as many strangers as possible to see if they'd be interested in a business like that.

"If that cat food thing doesn't work out, let me know if you want to sell vitamins. For people, not cats," he said with such a goofy laugh, that I didn't take offense.

"Thank you." I tucked his card into my pocket.

The cashier called out, "Number 46."

"That's me," I said, grabbing my pizza box. "Have a good night."

He moved out of the way and then held the door open for me. "Maybe I'll see you at the market next time." His big hands reminded me of a puppy with oversized paws that he hadn't grown into yet.

I was pulling into my driveway when Yollie called to fill me in. "Benson had two phones," she said. "Norma said one of them was a burner phone."

Wow. "That's interesting," I said. "Did Steven remember seeing it?"

"Not really," she said. "But that's not something he'd pay attention to."

"Where did she find it?"

"That's the strangest thing," she said. "She made the crime scene people go back and search the house again and they found the phone and some money in a hiding place under the floorboards."

"That *is* strange," I said. "Did she have any idea why he was hiding it?"

"No, but she seemed mad at the crime scene guys because they should have found it during the first search. I guess the phone was used for only one number and that phone is turned off now. If they found it earlier, maybe they could've learned something from it."

"Did she tell you anything else?"

"That's all I can remember," she said, and we hung up.

I pulled out the cat carrier and the pizza and headed inside, my thoughts swirling. Why did an oboe teacher need a burner phone?

"Pizza!" Elliott yelled. Then he added ultra-politely. "Hi Mom. How was the farmers' market?"

"Fine son." I mimicked his tone. "How was rehearsal?"

"Great!" He took the pizza from me while I opened the carrier door for Trouble.

She took her time coming out and then stretched before following Elliott to the kitchen, meowing. *You forgot to pet me!*

"How much time do you have before your Power Moms meeting?" he asked, sliding plates across the table to set it quickly. "Grandpa! Pizza!"

"Shoot," I said. "I forgot about that." The Sunnyside Power Moms, or SPMs for short, was a group of home business owners who worked together to network and support each other. We met every month to go over joint marketing opportunities, especially at community events. "Buy Local!" had become our self-serving motto and we used the banner wherever we could.

"Do you have to go?" Elliott asked.

My dad walked down the stairs, a little glassy-eyed like he'd been napping. "Go where?"

"SPM meeting," I said. I was pretty tired from such a full day, but then I thought about Benson. That group of women was connected to lots of people all over Sunnyside and had been a good source of information in the past. "I better get going."

"Hey Mom?" Elliott asked, his voice tentative.

"Hey Elliott?" I responded.

"Is it okay if Da—Richard comes to opening night?"

After saying, "Of course," through clenched teeth, I grabbed two slices of pizza and put them on a paper plate, then dashed out the door.

I ate on the way there, wiping the pizza evidence from my lips before I went in. The current leader of the Sunnyside Power Moms was Gina Pace, a personal trainer, who also ran the Mommy and Me classes around town, and she probably wouldn't approve of my dinner. She had more energy than anyone I'd ever met. Yollie and I had become friends through SPM, but she wasn't at the meeting when I arrived late. The group was discussing our participation in the upcoming Sunnyside Elementary School Holiday Bazaar and debating whether we should spread our booths out or stay all clustered together. The spread out faction won.

Several of the moms sent me curious looks, and sure enough, as soon as the official meeting was over, they rushed over to ask me about Benson's death.

"Did you really almost die?" a new member asked. I'd forgotten her name and it seemed like a bad time to ask.

I guess that part of the story was leaking out, even though I hadn't seen Yollie's or my name mentioned on any of the news channels.

I told the group an abbreviated version of the story, and Gina said, "Are you looking into that death too?" Gina had previously helped me track down a murderer and took every opportunity to let people know.

"Oh no." I lied through my teeth. "Why, do you have any clues?" I said it jokingly, but she gave me a meaningful look.

"Ah come on, Gina," another mom insisted. "Tell us."

"It's nothing concrete," Gina said with a coy smile. Then she dished. "But I heard that the PTA president of the elementary school was very distraught at the news, even though a certain oboe teacher dumped her a while ago."

"Didn't she get divorced last year?" someone asked.

Another mom protested, "She's single now. She's allowed to date. What's the big deal?"

Gina shrugged. "If it wasn't such a big deal, then why keep it quiet? Also, it seems that the oboe teacher had a thing for recently divorced moms."

A couple of women gasped. "He was taking advantage of them?" one asked.

Gina shrugged. "That's what I heard." She turned to me. "The PTA meeting is next Monday evening, at the elementary school. You know, if anyone wanted to, I don't know, they could stop by to talk to her."

She followed that up with a smirk but I acted nonchalant. I'd learned the hard way that letting all of Sunnyside know I was investigating a murder was never a good thing.

Chapter 9

Welcome clouds had started moving into the area overnight and a few drops were falling by the time I pulled into the parking lot at the commercial kitchen the next morning.

This was cause for celebration in southern California after so many months of no rain, and I smiled as I let the drops hit me.

One of the bakers was getting out of his car too. "Makes you want to dance to that 'Singin' in the Rain' song, doesn't it?"

I spun around in a circle with my arms out and he shook his head at me.

"I was kidding," he said, holding the door for me.

Zoey was standing at the metal counter, staring at the schedule, but I wasn't sure if she was actually seeing it.

I was so used to seeing her full of energy but not today. "Did something happen?" I asked.

She shook her head. "Later," she said.

Then two police officers walked in and her eyes grew wide. They asked for me and when someone pointed, they walked over holding a clear plastic bag filled with the kitchen tools that had been confiscated in the search.

"Does this mean you didn't find the murder weapon here?" I asked but they were just the delivery people and didn't know.

Quincy was in his office, so I went upstairs to ask him. "Good morning," I said. "Did you see that? We got all the kitchen utensils back. That's good news, right?"

"Seems to be," he said.

"Yay. None of them were the murder weapon. I'm so surprised," I said in my most sarcastic tone. I plopped down into one of his chairs.

"Me too." He smiled and leaned back in his leather chair, with his arms behind his head. "We just have to be patient until the police make some kind of statement. That won't happen until the yogi returns from India."

"After all that hoopla, they should do it sooner rather than later," I grumbled.

Quincy changed the subject. "How are things going with Twomey's?"

We discussed the upcoming order and his ideas for next quarter's marketing. I thought about giving him a hint about Zoey's predicament, but I had to ask her first. She was very independent and proud. Getting her to take any help was going to be difficult. I didn't want to make her defensive right off the bat.

By the time I made it back downstairs, Zoey had put away the kitchen tools. "So what does it mean?" she asked.

"I'm not sure," I said. "Let me call Norma." I dialed, keeping an eye on Quincy's office to make sure he didn't hear me. As far as he knew, I was staying out of it. "Time for coffee?" I asked when Norma answered.

"Sorry, not today," she said.

"Oh. Um, I see that our kitchen stuff was returned. I'm assuming that means none of them were the murder weapon, which *we* all knew."

"That's true," she said.

"So did you find it?" I tried.

"Yes."

"Whoa."

"Yes. Whoa." She sounded sarcastic.

This wasn't getting me anywhere. "Can you tell me what it was?"

"No," she said.

"We were thinking it might be a mandrel," I said.

"Oh really?" Her cold tone made me think that I might be on the right track.

"If that's true, then the murder wasn't all that planned out, right? The murder weapon was just sitting there, conveniently. Anyone could have picked it up and used it."

"What are you trying to say?" she asked.

"Just that the whole theory of how Quincy could have done all that like some kind of criminal mastermind doesn't work," I said.

"Have a nice day," she said and hung up.

Zoey was looking at me wide-eyed. "What did she say?"

"Not much," I said.

"Wow. Sounds like she shouldn't mess with you." She wiggled her shoulders in an *ain't you something special?* move. "You sounded like that *Serial* podcast, clearing innocent people accused of murder."

"You ready to tell me what's going on?" I asked and regretted it immediately when she started crying. "I'm so sorry! I'm an idiot. Just ignore me."

She shook her head. "I'm the idiot." Her shoulders moved in silent sobs, and the other workers in the kitchen began to notice.

"Let's go," I told her. Then I yelled out to the other staff. "We'll be back to clean it up."

We walked out the back door to one of the wooden picnic tables near the loading dock.

"Tell me everything," I said.

'Okay," she said. "Really, it's kind of your fault."

I could tell she was joking, but I still blinked a couple of times.

"I was going around in circles for hours yesterday until my brain said to me, 'What would Colbie do?'" she said with a small, sad smile.

"Oh no," I said.

"And I decided that I should send my friend to the bar Red always goes to and see if they can find out what he's up to."

I thought of the sexist way he'd treated me, someone he didn't know. "A friend who's male or female?"

"Oh male. Definitely," she said. "He bought Red a drink and got him talking and he found out his 'grand plan.'"

"What is it?"

She took a deep breath. "He moved back in with his mom and he got a lawyer to take his case pro bono. He's going to fight me for partial custody and then he's going to make me pay child support." Her voice broke at the end.

"Well, that'll never happen," I said. "What judge in his or her right mind would give that lunatic any amount of custody?"

She pressed the heels of her hands into her eyes. "You don't know him. He's going to charm the pants off his lawyer, and then charm a judge, and he's going to get my baby."

"No, he won't," I said. "I have the videotape of him losing his mind."

"He'll have some excuse that everyone will believe because he's so pretty," she said and then sat up straight. "But he's not going to get my Zeke. Ever. I'll kill him first."

I looked around, making sure no one could hear her. "Zoey, don't ever say that out loud again. And don't do it either. What would happen to Zeke, or Meowio, if you were in jail?"

She smiled a little at my joke, but I wasn't sure I got through to her.

"Did you do anything to make him go away?" I asked.

"I gave him five thousand dollars, all the money I had," she said.

"Do you have proof of that?" I asked.

She shook her head. "It was all in cash."

"Let's wait for the lawyer to actually do something," I said. "Or maybe he was making the whole thing up and he was just talking big."

In the meantime, I had to find a time to let Quincy know what was going on. He had his own problems, but he'd be awfully mad if he found out what was happening to Zoey from someone else. And he was a smart guy. He might have a solution.

* * * *

Elliott refused to go to the Sunnyside Library Family Movie Night with me since according to him, *it was for babies*. I thought about going alone, but that was not only weird but pretty pathetic. And it would definitely make it harder to get Mad Dad to talk to me.

I texted Joss, including the real reason I wanted to go, and he called me right away. "Really, you're using me and my daughter to track down a suspect?"

"Oh man, I didn't think about it that way," I said, completely embarrassed. "You're right, forget it. Sorry!"

I was about to hang up when he said, "I'm kidding. What can happen at a library movie night?"

Trouble looked up from my lap and meowed as if she had heard him. *You don't want to know.*

She purred while I read over what Mad Dad, or Fred Hugo, had posted on Benson's Facebook page. He'd publicly admitted to obtaining a copy of his daughter's recommendation letter from Benson, by requesting a paper copy in a sealed envelope for a college that requested them by paper. I didn't know much about applying to college, but I couldn't imagine any college taking paper these days. Mr. Hugo had read the letter and complained that it wasn't good enough, that it contained so-called "code" words like "hardworking," which inferred that his daughter wasn't that talented.

What ensued was a debate on how illegal that was and how inappropriate it was to be discussing this on Benson's Facebook page. I couldn't imagine that any of it helped his daughter get into college, never mind the teen humiliation she must have suffered from his public display. Benson never commented on the post, which must have taken some restraint, or he just didn't care.

Joss knocked on the door and we drove over to the library. The rain had stopped, but more was expected over the weekend. The amount that had fallen was only enough to promote more growth, which just gave any fires more fuel. We needed a thorough soaking.

Movie nights at the Sunnyside Library were way more popular than I expected. The parking lot was packed so Joss dropped Kai and me off at the door.

Kai held my hand and skipped as we went inside. "I already taught Percy how to give me a high five," she said. "Well, he doesn't do it every time, but it's only been a couple of days. Pegasus hardly does it at all."

"Cool," I said, impressed. "What other tricks are you going to teach them?"

"I'm going to teach them to come when I call them, and dance in a circle, and jump over each other." She used her hands to demonstrate and nodded as if it was definite.

Then she told me she *loved* the movie, *Mulan*. The whole night was made even better for her when she saw some friends from school. She excitedly joined their group sitting on the floor in front of the big screen in the center of the library.

Joss and I sat with the row of parents in real chairs at the back of the room. I had printed out the photo of Fred Hugo, aka Mad Dad, and discreetly opened it to compare it to some of the dads in attendance. It took longer than I expected to find him because the lights were dimmed in the library and his photo was pretty outdated. I finally figured out who he was when he lumbered to his feet and set off for the men's room.

"Go in there and talk to him," I hissed at Joss.

He stared at me like I was nuts. "I'm sure that happens all the time in the women's room, but men don't talk to strangers in the men's room."

"Oh," I said. "Okay. You stay here. I'm going to catch him when he comes out." On the way, I realized that my normal tactic, flirting, wasn't such a good idea at family movie night.

I'd have to be straightforward. "Is that you, Fred?" I asked when he exited the bathroom, waving his hands in the air to dry them off.

He looked at me, trying to remember if he knew me. "I'm Colbie. Someone told me that your daughter used to be taught by Benson Tadworth. I'm so sorry for your loss."

His face turned bright red at the sound of Benson's name. "Thank you, but she hasn't been with him for a while."

I nodded sympathetically. "I heard he could be a real pain."

"Yeah," he said. His hands tightened into fists.

"I overheard him with a student just a couple of weeks ago," I said. "He was terribly abusive."

"Um, I should get back to my family," he said.

I grasped at straws. "Do you know any other teachers who don't use such awful methods?"

"No," he said, his voice firm. "What was your name again?"

"Colbie."

"Well, Colbie," he said, "I don't like to speak ill of the dead but Benson Tadworth was a horrible human being and he—"

It was pretty clear that he wanted to say, "...deserved what he got." Then he thought better of it.

"I have to get back to my family," he said and turned around.

I wasn't going to get anything more out of him, but maybe Norma should make sure he had a rock solid alibi.

* * * *

The Little Italy Farmers' Market on Saturday extended for blocks close to downtown San Diego. The local neighborhood was filled with restaurants and art galleries, and from some streets we could see San Diego Bay.

I covered my tables and set up all the products before getting Trouble out of her cat carrier and putting the chef's hat on her. She held court on her chair and drew her normal crowd.

Today I was on my own because Elliott was at rehearsal. The weather felt perfect—crisp and cool—but the highly anticipated rain was scheduled to move in later. I planned to use that as an excuse to close up early so that I could attend Benson's memorial.

I saw the nutrition pyramid scheme guy before he saw me, strolling down the aisle of booths. Today, he looked more casual, wearing a green golf shirt that he'd tucked into khaki pants. His dark hair was standing up in the back, as if he hadn't bothered to get his cowlick under control.

I gathered all of my patience, reminding myself that he was most likely here as a potential new customer and wouldn't be trying to push me into his business.

"Fancy meeting you here," Drake called out with a short donkey laugh.

"Welcome to my booth." I hoped my Vanna White hand gesture made up for my stiff smile.

He stared at Trouble for a minute. "Wow. That's a real cat."

"That's Trouble, my taste tester and the inspiration behind Meowio Batali."

Trouble stared at him as if wondering why he wasn't petting her.

"Cool hat." He picked up a can of my Chicken Soufflé. "Just like on the can. That's awesome branding, man. Who can forget that?"

"Thanks," I said.

"So what makes this better for my cat?" He turned it around to read the ingredients.

I went into my spiel and he nodded, listening intently. Then he completely changed the subject. "How much do you pay for this booth? Maybe I should rent one and sell my stuff here."

"Um," I said. "There's an info booth out front that can help you with that." I pointed in the general direction of one of the entrances to the market.

"Cool," he said. "So what should I buy for my cat?"

He bought a sampler pack and seemed ready to ask another question, but instead he said, "Thanks! I'll be back next week if Dijon likes it."

"Cute name," I said, relieved that he wasn't starting his own sales pitch. "Good luck."

He melted into the crowd and I heard Kai's voice. "There she is!" I turned to see Joss arrive along with Kai. She was holding a hot chocolate piled high with whipped cream. A tiny bit had landed on the sleeve of her red jacket.

"Wow!" I said. "I'm so lucky to get to see you guys twice in one weekend."

"Yes," she said, matter of fact about the compliment. "My mom's taking pictures of the goats for Instagram." She used a plastic spoon to push whipped cream into her mouth.

I raised my eyebrows at Joss. "Isn't that nice?"

He rolled his eyes. "Yep." His voice was tight. "It seems that baby goats are hot right now and Gemma thinks she can make some money with that."

I had no idea how people made money on Instagram, but then, my account was handled by Elliott and one of Quincy's public relations folks.

"Mom put them in pajamas today!" Kai said, as if she couldn't believe it. "They looked so cute."

"Baby goats in pajamas?" I kept my tone light. "I might even look at those pictures."

"Good," Kai said. "'Cause she needs lots of followers."

"Don't we all," I said. That was *so* not happening.

Kai moved over to pet Trouble, who arched her back and meowed. *It's about time you pay attention to me.*

"Did you leave because Gemma was there?" I asked Joss when Kai was out of earshot.

"How could you tell?" His voice was sarcastic. "She's hashtagging my farm, saying it'll help my brand. She's driving me nuts."

I don't know what got into me, but I had to say it. "Lani thinks Gemma wants to get back together with you." I held my breath.

"What?" He stared at me like I'd grown another head. "No way."

"Really?" I said. "This whole goat Instagram thing is pretty convenient."

He thought about it for a minute and then shook his head. "Impossible. She's dating some rich Canadian guy. Besides, I wouldn't take her back in a million years. She's the mother of my child but she's"—he cut himself off—"not a nice person."

I tried not to let the relief show in my face. "So, how long do you have to be away from home?"

He looked at his phone. "She just sent a text that she's done, so I guess it's safe now."

"Thanks for the nice surprise," I said.

"I do have the best surprises," he said, with a suggestive smile.

"Promise?" I asked. Then Kai came back over, sipping the last of her hot cocoa. "Will I see you at bowling?"

"Wouldn't miss it," he said.

"Will Elliott be there?" Kai asked.

"Oh yeah," I said. "He wouldn't miss it either."

They walked away and I watched them weave through the crowd. Saturday crowds were usually more mellow than during the week, taking their time to explore what was available in the different booths.

I turned around and scanned the crowd coming down the hill and noticed one person not moving. He was staring right at me.

It was Red.

Chapter 10

I fumbled bringing my phone out of my back pocket, dropping it on the table, and knocking over a stack of Seafood Surprise before turning on the camera app. By the time I looked back at Red, he was gone.

That was scary. Even surrounded by people, I was nervous.

I'd already been planning on packing up early so I could make Benson's memorial in time, so I tried to convince myself that a little earlier would be okay. Red was probably looking for Zoey, but he was such a bully that maybe me leaving early would make him feel good. That thought forced me to stay another hour, but I never saw Red again.

Funerals were often a great source of clues, but Benson's was so small, that I didn't know what I'd be able to find out. It was held in the Sunnyside Funeral Home and a local pastor greeted everyone as we entered the room where the service would be held.

According to Benson's obituary, his mother was his only living relative. She'd driven down from Orange County and sat in the front row, so distraught that there was no way I could approach her.

Losing a child had to be the most terrible thing that could happen to a parent. My heart clenched every time she cried through the short service. She had to have been supportive of her son. I saw what Yollie did to help Steven. I couldn't imagine anyone achieving what Benson did without his parent's backing.

I was surprised that Norma wasn't there, but a young man sat in the back, paying attention to everyone with the intentness of a police officer. He was sure to report back to her.

I'd kind of expected Opal Volker to be there, but Steven had seen her only one time. Maybe their relationship wasn't very serious.

Steven attended with Yollie, along with several other teens and their parents. I assumed they were Benson's students. Steven seemed sad but he had the presence of mind to speak quietly to Benson's mother. She gripped his hand tightly, and then pointed to some scrapes and smiled. I made a point of looking at the other students' hands. They all had Band-Aids and scars.

Yollie came to stand by me during the reception in a side room. "This is a little sad," she whispered. "I expected a lot more people."

"Do you think this will help Steven and the others get, I don't know, closure?"

"I hope so," she said. He was standing with other students, all in some level of formal dress that made them seem older, yet they fidgeted like normal teens.

"Do they all have scars on their hands?" I asked.

Yollie nodded. "Yeah, from making reeds."

Talk about suffering for your art.

* * * *

The promised rain held off until we were on our way to the bowling alley. Then the skies opened with a vengeance. I insisted on dropping my dad and Elliott off at the door. I still remembered the scary time when my dad could barely breathe because of pneumonia, and didn't want him to suffer like that again.

Piper would've told me that he couldn't catch pneumonia from getting wet, but I wasn't taking any chances.

My dad had snagged Joss for his bowling league months before, and Elliott and I were happy to tag along. Kai usually joined us on her dad's weekends. The rest of the team was around the same age as my dad, and many of them were from Boston like him. His Boston accent became more pronounced as the evening wore on, and the empty beer mugs piled up.

Elliott and I often played our own games, but tonight we were content to watch and eat junk food with Kai. My dad plopped down on the round couch in the viewing area at the end of the lane. "How was rehearsal?" he asked Elliott.

I'd already gotten the rundown and didn't pay much attention to his answer.

"That's a lot of work you guys are doing, all for one weekend," my dad said.

I was about to explain the reason for the short schedule, but Elliott handled it.

"Yeah," Elliott said. "Thanksgiving is early this year and that's the only time that was available at the high school. Plus, according to the drama teacher, it's the whole process that's important, not just the number of shows."

"Really?" my dad asked.

"No." Elliott laughed and shook his head. "But we're doing five shows in four days, so that'll be cool."

"I can't wait to see it," Kai said. "Especially the elephants!" She lifted her arms up above her head as far as she could reach. "My mom's coming to see it too!"

"That's great," I said, and Elliott turned his head fast to look at me. "Really," I said with a stiff smile, and he laughed.

"Hey, do you know what 'goat' stands for," Kai asked. "Greatest. Of. All. Time!"

"Very cool," I said. "I think you're the G.O.A.T."

She giggled. "That's what my dad says!" She threw herself back on the couch.

My dad pulled some money out of his pocket. "You kids want to play video games?"

"Sure," Elliott said, happily taking the money. They ran to the small enclosed video section, arguing on the way about which game they'd play.

My dad looked over his shoulder and saw that Joss was out of earshot too. "You know you gotta watch out for her, right?" he said. "That Gemma."

"Lani thinks so," I said. "But I asked Joss and he doesn't even like her."

My dad's eyes widened. "You asked him?"

"Yeah," I said slowly as if admitting something wrong. "Why?"

"I don't know," he said. "I just thought your generation played more games than that."

It wasn't clear whether he thought it was good or bad that I hadn't.

Then he gave a big dramatic shrug. "Sometimes, with men, it's not a matter of liking someone, okay?" He obviously felt uncomfortable telling me this.

Great. My dad wanted to talk to me about outdated gender roles, and worse, sex. "I know, Dad. You don't have to say anything else." *Please don't say anything else.* "We're good."

He nodded and patted my shoulder. "Okay. Just be careful with that one."

* * * *

On Sundays, I usually tried to get as much of the office work for Meowio done as possible. I handled the accounting, paid quarterly taxes, updated files, and made sure the marketing being done by outside people was on schedule. Today, I felt out of sorts and too antsy to sit inside, so after a quick run and a shower I took a ride over to Benson's house, back to the scene of the crime.

The garage was still taped off with crime scene tape and the house looked smaller than I remembered. Of course, at the time I'd been filled with anxiety about apologizing to Benson and then filled with even more anxiety that we all might die.

I walked around the garage and looked for the exit through the hedge that Norma had mentioned. The backyard was squishy from the rain the night before. Several feet inside the hedge ran a short wooden fence that circled three sides of the property. I opened the gate and as soon as I got close to the hedge, I could see the slanted path that ran through. It reminded me of Diagon Alley in the *Harry Potter* novels, minus the wands.

I went through to the other side and thought about last week when I'd first arrived there, looking for Benson's house. A BMW had been parked. Had the driver been trying to find Benson too? That didn't make sense. A minivan had brought the next student. Perhaps the driver's GPS had been messed up like mine and he or she was headed somewhere else entirely?

I turned around and found a string that opened the gate from the other side. Once I was through the hedge, it was easy to get into Benson's backyard. How many knew the somewhat magical way in?

I decided to ask Steven if anyone stopped by the morning I was there, the same time the BMW was parked. If so, he or she knew the way in and out, just like the killer.

I stopped at the grocery store and got home in time for one of Elliott's guitar lessons from my dad. Musical competence had skipped a generation in our family, but Elliott was making up for it.

"Can you show me that B chord again?" Elliott asked.

Elliott stared intently at my dad's fingers when he demonstrated. Then he bit his lip and stretched out his pinky finger, lightly making the same note. I knew he'd practice like crazy until he mastered it.

"What's the next song you're learning?" I asked.

"'I Want to Hold Your Hand' by the Beatles," Elliott answered.

I tried not to read anything into that, but I was definitely going to ask my dad who chose it.

I left them alone and texted Yollie. *Can I ask Steven a couple of questions about that day at his lesson?*

Sure, but he was just about to start practicing, BECAUSE TABITHA CHOSE HIM AS A STUDENT! she texted back.

CONGRATULATIONS! I texted along with emojis of balloons and champagne bottles. *Can I call now?*

She texted back *Yes*, and I dialed.

Steven answered his mom's phone.

"Congratulations!" I said. "That's great news about Tabitha."

"Thanks," he said. "I'm still kinda stunned."

"Well, you worked so hard and deserve it," I said. "Thanks for taking the time to help me. I know you want to practice."

"No prob."

"Do you remember anyone else at Benson's on the morning I picked you up?"

"No."

"Did he act different at all that morning?"

"No, except when he got mad at you."

Great. "No one knocked on the back door?"

"Nope." He was getting a little impatient.

"You said he got a phone call. Any idea who it was?"

"No, but Benson made his next student wait. I can't think of her name now. She's younger."

"You told me that you left your recorder behind. Did you listen to your recording from your lesson?"

"Yeah," he said.

"Any chance it taped what happened after you left?"

"I don't think so," he said. "But I only listened to my music."

I got excited. "Can you listen to it and let me know if you forgot to turn it off? Maybe it taped his phone call. It could be a clue."

"Okay," he said. "I'll let you know, but don't get your hopes up or anything. I usually turn it off when I'm done."

I still had my hopes up.

* * * *

Zoey was still low-key on Monday. She missed her son terribly and worried about how many days of school he was missing, but she couldn't risk Red finding him. Their nightly Skype video chats made Zeke feel better, but they made Zoey ache to hold him.

And Red had begun driving by all of Zoey's friends' homes, gunning the engine of his car in the early mornings. Zoey was moving around a lot, "couch surfing," as she put it and so far, she'd never been where he was causing trouble.

"They are going to get tired of dealing with him and kick me out," she said.

"You are always welcome on my couch," I said. "Or you can stay at Annie's house across the street. She has a lovely guest room and loves to have people stay with her."

She shook her head. "Thanks, but I'm good. For a while anyway."

I waited for her to be immersed in a recipe to sneak away to talk to Quincy. He was the richest, most powerful person I knew, and he'd do anything to help the people he worked with. He had a particular soft spot for single moms since his mother had raised him alone.

Feeling guilty, but not seeing a choice, I told Quincy what had happened in the parking lot, what Red's devious plan was, and how I'd seen him at Saturday's market.

He stroked his beard, deeply concerned.

"The worst thing is that he doesn't even want Zeke," I said, growing more indignant as I spoke. "He just wants to use him to get money out of Zoey."

"Have you told Norma?" he asked.

"Zoey won't let me," I said. "But she also didn't want me to tell you."

"I'm not sure what Norma would do, or recommend," he said. "Once he gets the legal system working on his custody, anything could happen."

"Zoey's worried that he can be charming when he needs to be," I said. He nodded.

"She said he's an anchor on her life, and that they're connected through Zeke," I said. "That's a chain she can never break."

He tilted his head, as if he had an idea.

"Maybe you can get him a job far away from here," I suggested.

"Colbie, he's dangerous." His voice was mild, but I heard the reprimand.

"Oh yeah," I said. "I guess we shouldn't inflict him on other people." I slumped down in my seat. "Maybe she just needs to lay low until he loses interest again." I really didn't like that plan. I wanted to take action.

Quincy shook his head. "Let me think on it."

* * * *

My regular Monday lunch with Tod went according to a pretty tight plan. After working in the kitchen in the morning, I would arrive at his apartment at as close to one in the afternoon as I could. Anything outside of a few minutes difference caused him so much anxiety that I erred on the side of getting there early and waiting outside until it was time. I brought sandwiches from the Vietnamese restaurant around the corner: shredded pork for Tod and chicken for me. Both sandwiches included the typical cilantro, pickled carrots and daikon radish.

While I waited for the right time to go upstairs, I glanced at my email and saw one from Norma that had the subject line *Dead end* on it. Was that cop humor? She let me know that Fred Hugo, aka Mad Dad, had a rock solid alibi for Sunday morning. He was a deacon at a local church and over fifty parishioners could verify that he was there all morning. So even though he had a lot of anger directed at Benson, he wasn't the killer.

Tod had opened his door and set up the table for our lunch. He was about my age, and just a few inches taller than me. With his brown hair and eyes and slight build, he could have played the sexy IT guy on any TV show, if he had any interest in acting at all.

His apartment was warm and nerdy and wonderful, with an overstuffed sofa in front of a huge gaming TV and shelves full of books and Star Wars action figures, along with other science fiction memorabilia. He had surrounded himself with the things he loved, and created a comfortable nest. No wonder he never wanted to leave.

His therapist insisted that our weekly lunches were helping Tod, and I was honored to be one of the three people he now let into his home, but sometimes his anxiety was so bad that his hands shook. I couldn't see how that much stress helped anyone.

We usually discussed the latest puzzles he was solving. He was addicted to puzzles of all kinds. Luckily, my investigations were some of his favorites, so he brought up Benson's murder before we opened our sodas.

"I looked up anything I could find about Benson Tadworth," he said, enthusiasm lighting up his eyes. "I started before you even asked me."

"Thanks," I said. "But how did you know I was even interested in him?"

"You and your friend were there, so I knew you might want to figure it out," he said.

I was about to ask how he knew that, since the police hadn't released our names yet, but Tod found things online that he shouldn't all the time.

"There's not much about Benson anywhere. He wasn't very technical." He said it like it was a foreign concept. "He just had that one Facebook page and a static website. And some nice SDHelp reviews."

"Static?"

"He hasn't changed it for five years," he said. "It's just his bio and how to contact him to arrange an audition."

"So you couldn't find anything?" I asked.

"Not much of interest except for a bunch of HOA complaints," he said. "The president of the homeowners association in his neighborhood sounded really fed up with him."

He turned his laptop around to show me the HOA membership page. "How did you get—? Never mind." I looked over the notifications that were sent to Benson. He never replied, on this page at least. "Whoa. They get a lot less professional as time goes on."

Tod nodded. "The president was pretty upset about the property not being kept up, especially the dead spots in the lawn."

I pointed to a message. "He seems to understand that Benson is just renting though."

"The owners of the house live in Europe. They rent to Benson, and the lease says it's the tenant's job to keep it in the same condition as it was rented," Tod said. "But he wasn't following through. According to the complaints, Benson dropped the gardener down to once a month instead of once a week. And the paint was chipping on the house."

"I guess I better go talk to this HOA president," I said. "Maybe he takes his job just a little too seriously."

Chapter 11

I met with oboe teacher Tabitha Higgins at Honey's Bistro in Encinitas. As soon as I saw orange and raspberry pancakes on the colorful, handwritten menu on the wall, I knew I was getting a second lunch. Or breakfast. Or breakfast for lunch.

Encinitas was a traditional beach town north of San Diego, and featured Moonlight Beach, one of the most popular beaches anywhere around San Diego.

Honey's was right in the middle of South Coast Highway 101, a street filled with quirky art galleries and ocean-themed shops. I parked a couple of blocks away and spied a guitar painted fun colors with tiny dinosaurs glued to it—definitely not for playing—and assorted mermaid statues, T-shirts and cute bumper stickers that said things like, *Instant Mermaid. Just Add Water* in store windows on the way. Surf shops were on every block.

According to Yollie and Steven, Tabitha charged more for her lessons and took a lot less students than other teachers. She'd been the lead oboist at the North County Symphony for almost ten years and planned to be there for twenty more.

I ordered my pancakes and soda at the counter and was given a number to take to my table.

I looked up at each person entering the restaurant, but my eyes slid right past Tabitha as she walked in. I assumed the tiny woman in the hippy bell-bottoms, ballet flats, and pixie haircut couldn't possibly be a world-class oboist until she stopped by my table. "Colbie?"

"Hi Tabitha." Even though I was average height, I felt like a giant when I stood up to shake her hand. This was the first time I felt like I should believe in fairies. Although the serious expression on her face wasn't anything I'd expect to see on a fairy.

She slid into the booth across from me and crossed one leg under the other with the ease of a teenager. Definitely a fairy.

"Thanks so much for meeting me," I said.

The waiter brought her a mug and filled it with fresh coffee. "Hi Tabitha." She must be some kind of special regular because everyone else had to order at the counter to get a mug and fill it from one of the huge urns along the wall.

"Hi," she said, staring at the coffee until he finished. Then she stirred in one Splenda, and carefully poured in creamer, stopping twice to stir and evaluate before pouring in more. Finally, she seemed satisfied and set her spoon down on her napkin.

She looked up at me and I noticed her caramel-colored eyes. Such an unusual shade. "What would you like to ask me?" she asked, getting down to business right away.

"I'm just learning about the whole oboe playing thing," I said.

She frowned, her mouth making a perfect sad emoji face. I must have sounded a little flippant.

I rushed on. "I'm looking into Benson Tadworth's death and I'd like to learn more about his life as an oboist and an oboe teacher. Like, why do you believe he chose to play the oboe?"

"Because it's a beautiful instrument," she said. "It's extremely challenging but when you master it, it's like making magic." Passion sparkled out of her eyes.

"What kind of person decides to make their career as an oboist?" I asked.

"It's not a career, like being in banking," she explained. "It's an obsession. It truly has to be the one and only thing you can consider doing with your life, or you will not overcome all the obstacles."

The waiter brought my pancakes. "What kind of obstacles?" I took a bite, hoping she'd talk for a long time. Oh man, they were delicious, sweet enough from the orange pieces and ripe raspberries that they didn't even need syrup.

"First of all, you are blowing a great deal of air through a tube the size of a blade of grass. That's extremely difficult even without making the correct notes. Then there are techniques you have to master like special breathing, double-tonguing, microtones, etc." She waved a hand like she could go on forever. "And your entire performance depends on this tiny reed. You spend years working on your reed-making technique, but there's no such thing as perfecting it. Even today, only thirty percent of my reeds are good enough to use and their effectiveness, which determines everything about my performance, is based on factors I can't control, like the barometric pressure at the time of the concert."

"Then why take it on?" I asked.

She leaned back and breathed deep, and her whole body seemed to fill up. She smiled. "Because when everything actually works and you make this beautiful sound that joins with the rest of the orchestra, it's an amazing feeling, like heaven on earth."

Then her food arrived—a salad with a large amount of seared ahi tuna on top. The dressing was on the side, along with a fruit salad filled with chunks of watermelon, cantaloupe, blueberries, and strawberries. She dipped her fork in the dressing and then stuck it through one piece of ahi and a bunch of green lettuce leaves.

I waited for her to chew a bit before asking, "Do you think that's why Benson chose the oboe?"

She swallowed. "I didn't know him very well, but I imagine that's why we all chose it."

"I'd heard some things about his teaching style that I want to discuss."

Her face grew still, and then she turned back to her salad.

"His teaching methods were a bit drastic," I said. "For lack of a better word."

She nodded. "Yes. He believed in negative reinforcement more than positive."

"Did that cause problems for him or his students?" I asked.

She finished chewing the bite before answering, giving herself a minute to think. "His methods worked for some students but not for others."

"Do you know of any students or their parents who hated him?"

She shook her head. "Not one hated him. He did have some issues with parents and students who expected better recommendations than he provided. That caused a great deal of ill will." She gave me a sharp look. "Not enough to justify murder."

I decided to step back from that discussion and come around another way. "What did you think of him professionally?"

"He was a masterful oboist," she said.

"I don't know how it works in your field," I said. "But for example, why do you have your job with the symphony and he didn't?"

She straightened up and got a haughty look on her face. "I am a better musician." Then she paused. "But he also had personality differences with a lot of people. And a big part of belonging to a symphony, to any group of course, is being able to get along with people."

"Anyone in particular?"

She sighed, knowing why I was asking. "No. Getting a position in a symphony is harder than getting to the NFL. So many pieces have to fall into place, on top of having the skill required. The right temperament is a big part of it. The right opening at the right time. People stay in their position for decades, which severely limits any opportunities."

"Can you give me an example about his temperament?" I asked, remembering that he threw a book of music when he became irrationally upset with Steven.

She took a breath. "There are many examples, but the one people talk about because it was so egregious, was the worst. Benson had an opportunity to play with the San Clemente Philharmonic Orchestra, along with one of the best oboists in the country. It was a celebration of Bach and the event was sold out. During the *Sonata in C Major for Oboe and Continuo*, something went wrong with Benson's reed. Normally, the oboist would do his best, or quickly replace it, but Benson became so upset that he stood up and Left. The. Stage."

She shook her head as if it was the worst betrayal she'd ever heard of.

"And that affected his ability to work with another symphony?"

"Yes, of course."

"Was Benson good at getting his students into the right college?" I asked. "I'd heard some were disappointed."

She hesitated. "To a certain degree."

"What do you mean?"

"I have to explain something. As an oboist, his reputation was his hoard of gold."

I nodded.

She turned to her purse and pulled out a small plastic envelope that she opened to get an eyeglass cleaning cloth. Then she meticulously cleaned her glasses before putting them back on her nose. She took the time to refold the cloth, tuck it back into the plastic envelope and back into her purse.

I thought about all of the little eyeglass cleaner cloths that were running around my car and office, but I could never find one when I needed it. Maybe I should be more like Tabitha.

"Last year, Benson wrote a glowing recommendation letter for a student who was not as exemplary as he gave people reason to believe. From the rumors I heard, the student had a deal with him that he would use the recommendation to get into college, but he wouldn't audition for any of the schools' music programs."

"Why would a college admit a student based on music but not make sure he played?" I asked, confused.

She leaned forward. "It showed that he or she had exceptional talent, commitment, follow-through, and lots of other skills that would make him a good student."

"Okay," I said. "Why would a student who loved to play agree to that?"

"To attend a good college."

"So you heard that Benson gave a student a better recommendation than he or she deserved." I was repeating everything she said, but I was trying to figure out why it was significant. "Why would Benson do that?"

"From what I heard, the student went against their agreement once he got into the university. When he auditioned for the school orchestra, it was clear to the artistic director that he wasn't as talented as Benson's letter claimed."

"So Benson hurt his reputation, or his hoard of gold, for this student," I summarized.

She nodded.

"Do you know why?"

She frowned. "For money, perhaps. The student's family is quite wealthy. It's not unheard of. Some people believe that he's done it before this and the students followed the agreement not to audition. Then no one would be the wiser."

"Would you do it?" I knew asking such a question was taking a risk.

"Of course not," she said. "Besides the integrity of the issue, Benson severely hurt his ability to help his other students get into that school. The orchestral director would never trust him again. If word got out, other colleges wouldn't admit his students. Then he'd stop getting students. It would result in a terrible cycle."

"How did you hear about this?"

"Our world is quite small. And very gossipy," she readily admitted

"So it was short-term thinking on Benson's part," I said.

She nodded.

"Could he have desperately needed money?"

She shrugged. "That's really all I know about it."

"Can you tell me the student's name?"

"Oscar Jenkins, as in Jenkins Industries."

The name stunned me. Jenkins Industries was a business consulting company that was big enough to put its name on a local community center. I couldn't imagine any family members having a difficult time getting into college. They could just buy a library or something and their kid was in.

I decided to stop beating around the bush. "Do you have any idea why someone would want to kill Benson?"

She shook her head. "Part of me feels like you're grasping at straws by looking at his oboe life. Perhaps you should focus on one of the more common reasons. He was quite the ladies' man. In college, he slept with the entire piccolo section."

About a thousand dirty piccolo jokes went through my mind, and I had a hard time not laughing.

Something must have shown on my face because she said, "Yes, he endured a lot of comments about the size of his 'piccolo.'"

"And he was still a ladies' man?" I asked.

"According to the gossip, he was even worse," she said. "I don't know how he finds the time. Our schedules are so constrained by our jobs. It's easier to date another musician."

I thought of something she could help me with. "How could I find out about his students, including those he may have let go?"

She thought for a moment. "I believe his Facebook page has his recital programs." She brought up the app on her phone. "Here." She turned to show me. "You can see his past events going back years."

I took her phone and made the words larger. The program listed students and the works they'd be performing. I made a mental note to dig deeper.

"Any reason you can think of that someone would be angry enough at Benson to kill him?"

She took the question seriously. "I don't know anyone specifically, but you have me thinking. I love playing the oboe more than I enjoy anything. I'm sure there are others like me. If Benson got in the way of them doing their life's mission? Maybe that could make them angry enough to kill."

Chapter 12

I got stuck in traffic in two different construction zones on the way home from Encinitas. Luckily my dad had made an omelet for Elliott, so I went up to change for the PTA meeting.

I took a few minutes to check out Benson's programs as Tabitha had suggested. The list of orchestral pieces the students were performing made me realize how little I knew about music. These kids had conquered pieces that I'd never even heard of by Beethoven, Bach, and Mozart.

Then I noticed that A&D College Consulting was the sole sponsor of Benson's last three recitals. Why would a college consulting company sponsor Benson's event?

If they were a sponsor, they had to know something about Benson. I needed to talk to them.

A&D's website was straightforward. They helped "Ambitious and Dynamic" students get into the college of their choice through SAT training, essay development, and organizing students' application schedules.

I clicked on the staff bios. Except for the owner, Ian Luther, who *might* be over thirty, all of the consultants were recent graduates of exceptional universities—Harvard, Yale, University of California, Berkeley, and more. All had helped an impressive number of students get into exceptional colleges in what had to be a short time in their career. Could those numbers be real?

They had three tiers of pricing, including "Specialized assistance with fees that varied."

It was time for me to find out what A&D could do to help my son get into the college of his choice.

Making an appointment with the owner wasn't as easy as I thought it would be. The admin answering the phone really wanted me to meet with one of the consultants instead, and I had to hold firm. Finally, she put me on hold and came back with an appointment on Wednesday afternoon. I said, "That works," and ran out the door.

Halfway to the elementary school, I heard and felt the "whomp-whomp" of a flat tire. Shoot. I dug through my wallet for my AAA Roadside Assistance card and called. Luckily, a tow truck would be able to help me in less than half an hour. Maybe I could still make the meeting. At least it wasn't raining.

I called my dad to let him know what was happening. "And don't remind me that you taught me how to change my own tire. I totally forgot and that's why I have AAA."

"I won't," he said. "I also taught you how to change your oil."

"Ha-ha." I hung up.

Soon, the driver pulled up behind me and I got out of the car to greet him. "How ya doin?" he asked. "Yep, that's flat." He felt around and pointed out a screw pressed into the rubber. "You need to take that in and get it repaired as soon as possible, like tomorrow. You gotta donut?"

"Yeah," I said. "In the trunk."

We worked together to pull it out and he expertly removed the tire. "Well lookee here," he said, and pulled what looked like a piece of electronics from the bottom of the car. It had a small antenna sticking out of it.

"Is that thing a tracker?" I asked, once I got past the idea that he was pulling off something essential to my car's engine.

He handed it to me. "Sure is. I seen these things before, but bigger than this," he said. "You owe somebody money or something?"

"What?" I was stunned. "No."

"Jealous ex?" the driver suggested.

I considered and immediately disregarded the idea of Richard tracking me. "No. Nothing like that."

He looked at me like he didn't believe me. "Well, you got some kind of trouble if you're driving around with that thing on your car."

My heart started racing and I set the tracker on the ground. Who the heck would be tracking me? My first thought was to call Norma, but instead I dialed Tod.

He answered right away. "Hi, Colbie," he said, sounding cheerful. "How are you?"

"I'm not sure," I said, while I watched the tow truck driver putting the donut on. I explained about the tracker.

"Can you send me photos of all sides of it?" he asked.

"Yes," I said. "Call me back when you know something." I hung up and did as he'd asked, taking photos from all sides. I used my sleeve instead of putting more of my own fingerprints on it, hoping the police would be able to figure out where it came from. I sent the photos to him and waited a minute to make sure they arrived. My phone was sometimes flaky about photos.

I was about to call Norma when Tod called me back. "You found something already?"

"Yeah," he said. "The bad news is that it's a very sophisticated, very expensive GPS tracker used primarily by the military."

"What the hell?" I asked. "Is there any good news?"

"Yes," he said. "It's used primarily by the American military."

"That's supposed to make me feel better?" I asked, my voice getting loud.

"Well," he said. "At least you're not being tracked by an international spy or something."

I shook my head. "I have to call Norma."

"I'll send her what I found out," he said. He'd met Norma when we were both suspects for a murder a few months earlier and they'd become friends too.

"Not yet!" I said. "She won't be happy that I called you first. I'll let you know when."

"Sure thing," he said. "I'll see what else I can find." He hung up.

The driver went back to his truck to fill out the paperwork and I looked at my car as if it had changed into something foreign.

I called Norma and explained what the driver had found.

"Did you touch it?" Her voice sounded serious.

"Yeah," I admitted. "The driver was wearing work gloves, but I wasn't. I dropped it pretty fast, though."

"Where are you?" she asked.

I told her.

"Tell the driver to stay put until I get there," she ordered.

"Sorry," I said to the driver when he returned with my AAA card. "The police are on their way and they want you to wait here."

"Yeah," he said. "That makes sense. Let me call it in. They're probably going to have me tow this baby to the station anyway."

Great. My car was now evidence. I stared at the photo of Trouble in her chef's hat that was plastered along the side of my little Subaru. How was this possible?

Then I looked down at the tiny piece of equipment at my feet, wondering if it had something to do with Benson. But how could an oboe teacher be involved with the military?

* * * *

The tow truck driver was right. My car had to be taken in for evidence. Norma gave me a ride home and wasn't helpful at all with providing any information or making me feel better. She was deep in her thoughtful mode and just kept responding, "Hmm," when I said anything. She was obviously not listening at all.

She came back to the present when we pulled up in front of my house. "I'll make sure you get your car back as soon as I can."

I wasn't sure if I believed her. Her commitment to solving the murder outweighed my inconvenience for sure. I didn't invite her in, the sight of my house making me feel like curling up in a corner with some tea and Trouble on my lap. I had enough of this intrigue stuff.

My dad was in his recliner, beer in hand, when I came in. He asked, "How was the PTA thing?" and I realized I still had time to make the end of the meeting.

Shoot. I so didn't want to leave, but if I didn't go tonight, I'd have to wait until next month's meeting. I put off telling my dad about the tracker and just asked if I could borrow his car.

He gave me a funny look, but said, "Sure," and threw his keys to me.

On the way, I called Quincy. "How are you holding up?"

"I'm fine," he said. "What's going on?" I tried not to call him outside of business hours so he knew it was important.

"Do you have any contracts or dealings with the military?" I asked.

"No," he said. "Not for any big reason. I just usually stick to businesses that deal with the general public. Why?"

I explained about the tracker on my car and he seemed stunned. "I can't imagine why someone would do that to your car."

"Yeah, it's not like it was mistaken for another Subaru with Meowio Batali Cat Food all over it."

"Exactly," he said. "Wait. Are you investigating the Benson murder?"

* * * *

I was happy to see that a handful of cars were still in the Sunnyside Elementary School parking lot when I arrived for the PTA meeting. I parked close to them, walked up to the front door and pulled on the handle.

It was locked. I held my hands up to peer through the window. The inside was dark.

Damn. I missed the meeting.

I went back to my car and heard voices from around the back of the building. I kept walking around the school and then I smelled something. Pot.

Without thinking, I peeked around to see who was behind the school smoking pot. And was surprised, gobsmacked actually, to see a bunch of PTA moms sitting on the green lunch tables, passing around a joint. Holy cow! I almost couldn't believe my eyes.

I could tell they were PTA moms by their Sunnyside Elementary School sweatshirts, the clipboards and folders they'd tossed on the tables, and the piles of wrapping paper samples for the fall fundraiser.

"Uh, hello," I said, coming out from behind the corner. "I'm looking for Freddie, the PTA president?" I couldn't help but end on a question mark. Even Miss Manners wouldn't know the proper etiquette for this situation.

"I'm Freddie." She said her name in two distinct syllables, obviously feeling very relaxed.

Another mom waved a hand at her. "Our fearless leader."

I gingerly moved closer and introduced myself. "I'm wondering if I could ask you questions about Benson Tadworth."

"Sure," she said. "His penis was—"

I interrupted her as her friends broke out into laughter. "No, not anything like that. Just like, what kind of person he was."

"Are you a reporter, 'cause this," she waved around the joint, "can't go in the paper."

"No." I gave an uncomfortable chuckle. "Definitely not a reporter, and I think that's fine. Really." I did not sound convincing. When did I turn into such a goody-goody? "Can you tell me anything about him?"

She made a scoffing sound and handed the joint to another mom. "Other than he was a class A douchebag? Not really."

"That's what I heard," I said to encourage her. "But the other person didn't give me any details. What made him a, you know, that."

"I'll have to introduce you to the We Hate Benson Tadworth Facebook group," she said, her dreamy voice at odds with what she was saying.

"A Facebook group? That's cool," I said, cringing inwardly at my suck-up tone. "How many members?"

She shrugged elaborately. "Twelve?"

"Wow, he really must be a…a jerk. What did he do to piss off that many women?"

"What didn't he do?" she said. "He met us all online, pretended to fall in love with us, convinced us that he was sincere, and as soon as we were hooked on him, he ghosted us."

"Like, never responded to your texts?" He really was a jerk.

"Yeah," she said. "Blocked us too."

"Did anyone confront him?" I asked.

"It took us a long time to realize we weren't the only ones," she said.

"Hey Freddie," one of the other moms said, "I gotta get home to my little urchins."

I took that as my cue to leave and handed Freddie my card. "Can you call me tomorrow to talk some more?" Although maybe she wouldn't be as forthcoming when she was sober.

"Sure," she said. "I have a lot more stories for ya."

I went back to my dad's car and started the drive home, wondering why they thought it was okay to smoke pot at their kids' elementary school. Would they drink a beer? Smoke a cigarette? Did the principal know? Maybe she was so grateful for the support of the PTA that she let it go.

Then the whole issue became moot as I saw flashing lights of two police cars pulling into the parking lot! I was already on the other side of the school and saw the moms scatter like teenagers at a rave. I couldn't resist pulling over to watch the drama unfolding right in front of me.

Unfortunately, some of the PTA moms were much slower than teens and were quickly rounded up by the four officers. I wondered if any of them would squeal on the others who got away.

I opened my window to hear better and Freddie scared the crap out of me by opening the door and getting in. "Drive!" she commanded, frantically swiveling her head to see what was happening back at the school.

Catching her urgency, I gave a nervous laugh and followed her order, heading away from the school.

"Did you call those police?" she demanded.

"No!" I said. "I was just there a minute ago. They would have got me too." Now they could only get me for aiding and abetting an escaped criminal.

"It seemed longer," she said, sounding unsure.

"That's the pot talking," I said.

She kept turning to look behind us and then staring at the rearview mirror. "I think we lost them." Her voice was breathless.

"Don't you think they'll check all the cars parked in the lot?" I said, trying not to laugh at her freaked-out expression.

Her eyes widened for a moment and then she breathed out. "Oh thank goodness I parked on the street."

I was pretty sure it was standard procedure for the police to check any neighboring cars to figure out who ran away, but maybe they'd settle for the slow-pokes they caught. I could just imagine the scandalous headlines tomorrow. And the gossip on the NextDoor app would be wild.

Freddie's phone rang and she pulled it out of her purse. "Grace? Are you okay?"

I could hear Grace clearly. Of course the fact that she was practically yelling helped. "I told you that was a bad idea! Why did you even bring it?"

Ooh that was interesting. The PTA president was the one luring the rest of the board into a life of crime. This was a Netflix series waiting to happen.

"Where are you?" Freddie asked. "Did everyone get away?"

I started to remind her that we saw people get caught, but she sent me a warning glance and held up her hand to stop me. Oh, she was *acting* dumb.

"No!" Grace sounded scared. "A bunch of your board members were arrested!"

"Like, actually arrested?" Freddie asked. "Maybe they were given a warning?"

"What is *wrong* with you?" Grace said.

"Well, I'm still a little out of it," Freddie said, but she had definitely sobered up by now.

"You mean 'high,'" Grace said. "You got your board high and then ran out of there like a scared rabbit."

Freddie didn't answer her. "I'm going to walk back. I'll let you know what I find out." She hung up in the middle of more of Grace's complaints.

"Sounds like you'll be having some trouble with your board members at the next meeting," I said.

"Yeah right," she said. "They all begged me to be president so they wouldn't have to do it. They can take my job anytime."

"Should I drive you home or do you want to risk going back to your car?" I asked.

"Let's go back," she said.

I circled the block to turn around. "It doesn't make a lot of sense to smoke pot on school grounds, you know."

"That's part of the fun," she replied, but seemed to be reconsidering that idea.

"You don't look like you're having fun now."

She didn't answer.

I realized I was wasting my time when I could be questioning her. I slowed down and she didn't seem to notice. "Hey, can you tell me more about the other women in your Facebook group? Was anyone more into Benson than the others? Like, did anyone make threats against him?"

We arrived on the block where she'd jumped into the car and she stared intently toward the school while I pulled over to make sure it was safe. "His latest ex sounded like the wrong person to cross," she said absentmindedly.

"Really? Who is she?"

"Her name is Opal and she's the counseling secretary at the high school. Not someone you want to get on the bad side of."

I almost jumped at the sound of her name. "Why not?"

"Well, Benson didn't have kids, so it didn't matter to him, but she could screw up your kid's application and you'd never know it. Or slow walk your recommendation requests. She has a lot of power. People don't realize that."

"Is she the kind of person to do that?" I asked.

"Oh yeah. Parents have been trying to get her fired, or at least moved out of that job, for years." She looked all around, I guess making sure no police were hiding.

"Do you want me to drive you to your car?" I asked.

At her nod, I pulled out. "What did she say about Benson that made her stick out to you?"

"She said she and Benson worked for the same person, and that she was going to royally screw him over."

What? Benson didn't work for anyone. He was a teacher and had his own quintet. Basically his own boss. Then I remembered the GPS tracker on my car. Maybe he did work for someone. Someone who was a little too interested in me.

I drove past the parking lot, which still held a few cars. I had a feeling they belonged to the moms who had been arrested. "Can you invite me to be part of that Facebook group?"

"Sure." She pointed to a burgundy minivan. "That's my car." She pulled out her phone and brought up her Facebook app. "What's your profile name?"

I gave her my full name and she found me. "Meowio Batali?"

"Yes," I said. "That's my company."

"Cute," she said while she typed away. "I sent you an invite. All you have to do is click it and you'll be able to see what everyone wrote."

"Can you think of anything else she said about who they work for?" I asked.

She shrugged. "She wished she was dating the boss instead."

"Why?"

"Because he had a lot of money and drove a great car," she said.

It looked like I had to go back to the high school again and talk to Opal.

Chapter 13

Elliott was in bed by the time I got home. When I checked on him, he was snoring, and I took his latest zombie book out of his hand and put it on his nightstand.

Before telling my dad about the GPS tracker, I softened him up with a comedic retelling of the PTA moms smoking pot and the arrival of the police. He actually had tears in his eyes from laughing so hard.

My voice must have changed, because his face went serious as soon as I started my story about the tow truck guy finding the GPS tracker.

I ended with, "So can you drive me to the rental car place tomorrow morning?"

He ignored my question and shook his head. "A GPS tracker? You have to stop looking into this murder."

"Dad," I protested. "We don't know for sure that it's connected. Benson was a freakin' oboe teacher, not an international hitman."

He frowned and pointed his finger at me, just like he used to when I'd done something wrong as a kid. "Don't give me that BS. You know it's connected. You just don't know how yet."

"Okay," I said. "Most likely, it is. That doesn't mean I should stop. There's been no, like, threat or anything."

He clenched his jaw and stared at me with narrowed eyes.

"Look, this time I'm giving everything to Norma," I said. "She's on top of it. It'll be fine."

I used feeding Trouble as an excuse to get away from his accusing eyes and found her sitting in the dining room staring at the small chandelier over the table. I agreed that it wasn't the most attractive light I'd ever seen. It was original to the house and resembled a six-legged octopus holding small candles. "You've seen that light a thousand times," I said. "Let's get you some dinner."

At the word "dinner," she hopped up to follow me and I took my time dishing out her Fish Romance, trying to think of some defense for continuing the investigation.

My dad quickly hung up the phone when I returned to the living room. Then he tossed me his keys. "I can use Annie's car if I need it," he said and turned the volume up on his TV show.

If I wasn't so tired after all that happened that day, I might have been offended at being dismissed. Instead, I was relieved that he wasn't arguing with me and went up to bed.

* * * *

The next morning, I was up early, waking with a jolt but unsure why until I remembered the tracker.

Disgusted, I went down to grab coffee and pulled out my laptop to check out the We Hate Benson Tadworth Facebook group. Instead, I got distracted by a bulletin about the Sunnyside Elementary School PTA.

Overnight, the news broke that almost the entire board, including Freddie, was arrested for smoking pot on school premises. I wondered how the police got her—did the others rat on her or were they waiting for her at home? The principal got involved and helped to make a deal that the moms would resign from the board in exchange for dropping the charges. I could just imagine that phone call to the principal. I don't think any training encompasses *how to handle PTA moms getting arrested for smoking pot behind your school.*

Besides, the punishment was making them resign? What was up with that? For a lot of moms, that was rewarding them for bad behavior. Would they get a free trip to Las Vegas if they embezzled PTA money?

But the deal was leaked somehow, and the news went viral. Pothead PTA Moms Burn Out was my favorite headline, and the rest of the country was having a great time making fun of the oh-so-California story.

Now the district attorney announced that he was reviewing the deal. Oh man. That couldn't be good.

I logged onto NextDoor and had never seen so many comments on one posting before. I didn't have time to read them all, but the consensus seemed to be a general condemnation of the PTA moms for breaking the law and being poor role models for the children who would hear about this.

One lone mom wondered which of the chastising parents was going to volunteer to replace them. I wasn't at all surprised to see that no one responded to her comment.

The next *Bad Moms* movie was writing itself.

I switched over to Facebook, bypassing a lot more "bad mom" postings to get to the We Hate Benson Tadworth Facebook group, and was almost late waking Elliott up with all the drama I found. The angry posts seemed to feed on themselves as more women joined in with their stories of abuse by Benson. If he wasn't dead, he'd be a poster boy for Man Who Should Be Banned From Every Online Dating Website. And warnings should be posted in women's bathrooms all over the city.

Everything Freddie had told me was reflected in the postings. Heartbroken women who had overcome a lot of cynicism and baggage to allow themselves to fall in love with the quirky, passionate musician who convinced them he'd finally found his match, only to dump them—without actually letting them know they were being dumped—once he'd conquered them.

The women were all very different physically—short, tall, thin, heavy, many different backgrounds—but they had two things in common. They were divorced and newly dating. And he took advantage of that, using the same combination of soulful artist and flattering companion on all of them.

If he wasn't already dead, I'd have wanted to kill him myself just for solidarity with women in general.

Fortunately for Quincy, but unfortunately for me, this Facebook group gave us a whole bunch of new suspects. I simply didn't have the bandwidth to look into all of them. And part of me felt like getting the police questioning these women was going to victimize them all over again. That was above my pay grade. Time to hand over the list of jilted lovers to Norma.

The only one I wanted to tackle on my own was Opal Volker. She'd scared me off before but I wasn't going to let her get away with that again. I texted Zoey to let her know I'd be in late and went straight to the high school.

I waited in my car in the faculty parking lot and saw her just as she was getting out of her small SUV. "Opal," I called out. "I'm glad I caught you."

She stopped walking toward the administration building and waited for me to get closer with a near-sighted squint that made me realize she didn't know who I was. As soon as I was close enough for her to recognize me, she turned around and started walking again.

I rushed to catch up. "I found out a few things about Benson that I need to discuss with you."

"I'm not telling you anything." Her tone teemed with malice, making me mad.

"Really?" I stopped walking. "Then maybe I'll just tell the police about your postings on the We Hate Benson Tadworth Facebook group page." I pretended to pull it up on my phone and read. "*I'll get him back. I'll get him back good.*" I tilted my head at her. "A little overly dramatic, but I bet a jury would eat it up."

She turned around and gave me a menacing glare. "You wouldn't dare."

"Just answer my questions and I'll go away," I said.

"Fine?" she said, impatience dripping from the word.

"Did he write recommendation letters for money?" I asked and then held my breath. I wasn't convinced that this would lead to murder, but it would help me figure out what kind of person Benson was.

"Yes."

"How do you know?"

"He told me," she said.

"You said that you and Benson worked for the same guy," I said. "What does that mean?"

She blinked at me, realizing the connection I was trying to make. Something flickered across her face that might have been fear.

"We both did freelance work on the side. What's the big deal?" she said.

"Who do you work for?" I asked.

She took a few steps toward me, and even though she was a few inches shorter, the malevolence on her face startled me to silence. "I don't need to tell you anything," she said. "You're not the police. If you come here again, I'll have you arrested for harassment."

* * * *

Somewhat shaken, I tried to make myself feel better by texting what I'd learned to Lani before I got on the road. My typing was a bit erratic, and I had to correct the autocorrect guesses more than a few times.

Lani must have sensed my distress, because she called me right away. "Are you okay?"

"Yeah," I said, although I didn't sound it.

"I didn't think so," she said. "What happened?"

It took me a minute to figure it out, but Lani waited patiently. "Opal confirmed that Benson wrote recommendation letters for money. But then she got really nasty. I wasn't going to let her scare me away again, but I think she's just naturally that mean. Talking to her made me even more nervous on top of what happened yesterday." I realized that I hadn't told her about the GPS tracker. "Oh man. You will not believe what happened."

"I already know about the GPS thing," she said. "Your dad called me last night. He wants me to stage an intervention."

"What?"

"Yeah." She laughed. "He thinks you might be getting too attached to these projects of yours. He told me to bring Piper as reinforcement."

"Right," I said but couldn't dismiss the idea that maybe I was in over my head. Again. But even after seeing the look on Opal's face, I had no intention of stopping. "He may have a point. I think I just talked to someone capable of committing murder. Maybe that's progress."

* * * *

Lani moved Opal up on the suspects list and suggested that I have Tod look into the possibly homicidal counseling secretary.

I called him on the way to work and he answered right away. "Maybe Benson was a spy," he said, sounding excited. "And that's why I can't find out much about him online."

"According to Tabitha, he's too busy for that," I said.

"Hmm, all those women." He sounded like he was considering it seriously as a problem to Benson being a spy. Hadn't he ever been to a James Bond movie?

He cleared his throat. "I know this is going to sound paranoid, but I think I should send someone over to check your house for bugs."

"What?" I tried to say, but it came out more like a squawk.

"Someone who is tracking your car could be the kind of person who tries other kinds of electronic surveillance." His tone was reasonable, but on top of everything else, it made my hands shake. I didn't answer him.

"Colbie?"

"I'm here," I said. "Let me think about it." I pulled into the parking lot of the commercial kitchen and was about to use it as an excuse to end the conversation but he didn't argue with me. "I wanted to see if you could look into Opal Volker." I explained why.

"Okay," he said. "But don't forget about my friend. You should have your house checked for bugs sooner rather than later." He sounded like a late night commercial for the local exterminators. "Also, I found out some information on that homeowners association president," he said.

I don't think I've ever been so happy to change the subject.

"His name is Marco Anderson and lots of residents have complained that he's a little overzealous."

"Aren't all HOA presidents overzealous?" In my opinion, anyone who had the time and energy to be HOA president had control issues. Or was a sociopath. Or maybe ran to keep the sociopaths off the board.

"I'm sending you his contact information," Tod said. "Even if he didn't do it, he might know another piece of the puzzle."

* * * *

I buried myself in cooking for a few hours, but couldn't stop thinking about what Tod had said. Should I have my house checked for bugs? What if his guy found one? My dad's house had become Elliott's and my true home. The thought of someone invading that sanctuary made my stomach ache.

Quincy came down and asked Zoey and I to join him upstairs once we were done with what we were working on. We finished shoving the finalized product into plastic bags, took them to the freezer, and stripped off our rubber gloves.

"What do you think he wants?" Zoey asked.

"Let's keep our fingers crossed that it's good news for a change," I said as we climbed the stairs.

"Come in, come in," Quincy said. "Anyone want a soda?" He opened the small refrigerator behind him. "Or an iced tea or kombucha?"

Zoey made a face at the last one. I totally agreed. "What's going on?" I asked.

Quincy turned his eyes to Zoey. "I want to help you."

She jutted out her jaw and looked at me. "You told him?" Her eyes were wide with betrayal.

"I had to," I said. "This is too much for you to take on yourself."

"That's not your decision to make." She stopped, too furious to talk.

Quincy raised his hand. "I have an idea. Maybe we can convince Red that he's not the father. Why don't you tell me if you think this plan will work?"

* * * *

Zoey hadn't forgiven me by the time we made it downstairs, but Quincy's plan had her intrigued enough that she didn't yell at me anymore. I was debating starting a new batch of Chicken Sauté when I received a text from Tod. I clicked on it.

Did you see Yollie's SDHelp review of the oboe teacher? He'd included the link and I clicked on it.

It was so over-the-top glowing that I had to stand up and walk around the kitchen, I was so angry. Why would she encourage other parents to have their children go through that abuse?

After letting Zoey know that I had to leave, and receiving a grunt in reply, I drove straight to Yollie's hair salon.

Yollie rented a spot at the Grateful Head Salon right on Main Street in Sunnyside. Luckily, she was waiting at the reception desk for her next client, beside the small mural of a Grateful Dead album cover that had a skeleton wearing a crown of roses. An unexpected look for a hair place.

Yollie didn't look happy to see me. "I'm waiting for a client," she hissed. The receptionist pretended not to hear her.

"I can't believe you gave"—I looked at the receptionist—"you-know-who a five star rating on SDHelp."

"Why don't you come back to my station?" she said. It wasn't a suggestion.

I followed her and she muttered through gritted teeth, "This couldn't wait until after work?"

"It seemed pretty important," I said. I leaned against her counter, resisting the urge to sit in the salon chair.

"Look. I could barely afford him. He offered me a ten percent discount to do that," she said with a huff. "It added up to a lot of money."

"He doesn't have very many reviews," I said. "And they're all positive. How is that possible given his teaching methods?"

"It's like everything in the arts," she said. "Do parents complain about *anything* in Elliott's theater groups? No, because they don't want to risk their kid not getting chosen in the future."

That was totally true. Parents put up with a lot and sometimes the people running the show took advantage of that. Which reminded me that I needed to focus some of my time on Benson's students. "Steven was going to look into students who weren't happy with Benson. How's that going?"

She narrowed her eyes. "He's been a bit busy. And there's probably a bunch of them."

I didn't have time for "a bunch." "Maybe we can bring them all together and make it seem like it's for another reason."

"You want Steven to lie to his friends?" She sounded horrified. "That's *so* not happening."

"If he gets me a list, I'll handle it myself and he doesn't have to be involved," I explained.

One of the stylists recognized me. "Hey, if it isn't Sunnyside's Sherlock Holmes." She laughed like it was the funniest thing in the world.

"You looking into that flute player's murder?" another one piped up.

I didn't bother to correct her.

"He played the oboe, you uncultured fool," the sole male stylist at the shop said before turning toward me. "Have you looked into his exes?" I just smiled.

An older woman client was examining the back of her razor cut hair in a mirror. "I bet it was the Deep State."

Her stylist rolled her eyes at me and pursed her lips like she was thinking hard. "You know, one of my Richie Rich kids clients said her dad paid someone a lot of money to help her get into college."

"Yeah, it's really expensive," I said.

"No, like he paid someone to write her essays, fill out her application, like, everything," she said. "It's not fair. The rich get richer, right? And they make sure their kids do too."

The male stylist nodded knowingly. "That's why there's so much income inequality. It's like the American caste system."

"Maybe someone was affected by chem trails," the client said. "And they just went a little crazy. You should check it out online. Our government is trying to kill us."

That's all I needed, to start going down conspiracy theory rabbit holes.

"I'll have to check that," I said, proud of myself for keeping a straight face.

The receptionist popped her head around the wall. "Yollie, your one o'clock is here."

Yollie pointed to the door. "Out."

Chapter 14

Coffee? I texted Norma and she texted back, *Yes. Twenty min.*

I'd skipped lunch so I added ricotta pistachio toast with honey drizzled all over it—my favorite food at Philz—to our coffee order.

Norma arrived exactly twenty minutes later while I was happily eating my food, the sweet and salty combination exactly what I needed. "That looks good," she said as she sat down. She took a long sip of her coffee before asking, "What ya got?"

"It's quite a mess," I warned her. "And it's not making much sense right now."

She leaned forward. "Really." She said it with anticipation, not as a question.

"Really," I said and then told her everything I'd uncovered. The pothead PTA president made her smile even though she knew all about it, but the We Hate Benson Tadworth Facebook group made her pull out her notebook. And my conversation with Opal Volker about her posting about going after Benson's boss had her shaking her head while she wrote.

To avoid being yelled at, I brought up Tod's suggestion that I have my house checked for electronic surveillance. She stopped writing and rubbed her eyes. "That might not be a bad idea."

I blew out a little breath. "Why?"

"We didn't get anything from the GPS tracker," she said. "No fingerprints. No serial numbers. Nothing to ID who put it there or where the info was going."

Holy cow. "When can I get my car back?" My voice sounded far away.

"Someone will return it tonight," she said. "You've been very helpful but I'd like you to take a step back from this thing. Now."

My heart was pounding and I didn't respond.

"I mean it, Colbie. I have a bad feeling about this. This investigation is sliding sideways, and I'm not sure where it's going."

I'd never heard her admit something like this before and found myself agreeing before I thought it through. "Okay."

She sat back in her chair, and then narrowed her eyes as if she didn't believe me.

"Can you tell me any status on Quincy?" I asked.

"Sure," she said. "If that will help you make the right decision."

I nodded.

"We found Quincy's yogi, but he's at a no-speaking retreat," she said. "And apparently, he takes that vow very seriously."

I laughed. "What about writing down his damn answers to your questions?"

She smiled. "That seems to be a no-go for him as well."

"Well, that sucks," I said.

"Yes, it does."

* * * *

My car was delivered that night by a young officer who insisted on handing me the keys himself. Someone had even washed it and found a decaying catnip mouse toy of Trouble's wedged under a seat.

I had really good intentions to take a break from the investigation, just like I told Norma. Especially after a wonderful evening with Joss that made me realize that I had it made.

Even though I'd made Joss laugh with the story of the pot smoking PTA moms, he'd become visibly upset when I told him about the GPS tracker. His reaction made me so nervous that I painted a much rosier picture of Norma's ability to find out who put it there than she'd told me.

It was the first time I hadn't told Joss the truth. Ever. So then I overcompensated by telling him that I was taking a step back, just like Norma asked me. That Quincy was about to be cleared as soon as his yogi started talking again, so there was no reason for me to continue.

And I meant it. The case was freaking me out. The fact that it was freaking out Norma and freaking out my friends and family was freaking me out even more.

And really, why was I running around risking so much when I could go about my wonderful life with my son, my dad, my boyfriend, my friends, and my business?

But the next morning something happened that really got me going.

Someone from A&D College Consulting texted me to say that the president, Ian Luther, was unexpectedly called out of town and they needed to reschedule my appointment with him.

Two hours before the meeting.

Sure, I'd forgotten all about the meeting. But that didn't matter. I was insulted. I called them immediately and no one answered the phone, so I left a barely polite message requesting a call back as soon as possible.

It occurred to me that Mr. Luther might be dodging me. Did he look me up? Maybe I should've used a different name. Instead of a call back, I received a text inviting me to meet in two weeks.

Whoa. They really were trying to avoid me.

What could I do? Drive there and see if the owner actually *was* out of town?

Then I remembered that Quincy had convinced me that Meowio was big enough to put on LinkedIn. It was just one of the ways I could put out good news for free, and a way to network with the other companies that were under his benevolent wing.

It also provided a way to search for people who used to work for A&D College Consulting. Perhaps an ex-employee would be willing to dish on them. I found a dozen people who no longer worked there, which seemed like a high turnover rate for such a small company, and decided to contact Jaxon Mason, a graduate of University of California Los Angeles who had left A&D four months before. She was now working at a private high school in Del Mar.

The school's website had everyone's extension listed which was a surprise, and Jaxon answered her own phone.

"Hi Jaxon," I said. "My name is Colbie and I was wondering if you had some time to answer a few questions about A&D College Consulting."

Her voice changed from friendly to wary. "Can you tell me what this is about?"

"I'm afraid I can't over the phone," I said.

She was quiet for a moment. "Then I'm afraid I can't meet you." She hung up.

I'd been hung up way too many times lately. I printed out her photo from the LinkedIn page, grabbed a backpack filled with books and a water bottle, and headed out to the school. It was much smaller than Sunnyside High School and seemed to be trying to look like an East Coast school, with red brick buildings and ivy climbing the walls.

The school had a very helpful website, which showed that the counseling office was in the administration building. And the administration building was on the square in the middle of the property. I waited on a park bench with a clear view of the door marked Counseling pretending to read a book.

I was about to give up when I saw Jaxon come out. She had the jaunty step of a young person leaving work and heading out for something fun.

"Ms. Mason?" I called out.

She turned toward me and looked like she was trying to place me. "Yes?"

"I'm Colbie," I said. "I called you earlier. I just need to ask you a couple of questions and then you never need to see me again."

Her eyes grew nervous and she looked around. "You're going to get me in trouble."

"With who?" I asked. The idyllic private school setting looked about as safe as the world could get.

She seemed to decide the same thing. "Are you with the police?"

"No," I said. "I'm a mom. I'm trying to help a friend who's in trouble. It's about Benson Tadworth."

She shook her head, as if at her own stupidity in helping me, and sat down beside me on the bench. "You have three minutes."

"What was Benson's connection to A&D College Consulting?" I began.

"The owner sent some of his clients to Benson, but I assumed it was because he was a great oboe teacher. The oboe is such an unusual instrument that it helped students get into college."

"But you don't assume it now."

She shook his head.

"Because he was murdered?" I asked.

She nodded slowly.

"Was there something funny going on at A&D?" I asked. "They cancelled a meeting with me at the last minute, and it feels fishy."

She grimaced and looked over her shoulder again. "That's one of the reasons I left, but they don't know that I know."

I moved a little closer. "What is it?"

"Ian, the owner, would meet this guy outside sometimes. He'd get a phone call, and then he'd go outside to meet him. And then he'd be all nervous before and after. It got me curious, so one time I followed him and saw him talking to a guy inside a luxury car, like a Mercedes or something. They talked for a really short time, like the guy just barked out an order to my boss. Then he drove off. It took Ian a few minutes to come back inside. Neither of them saw me."

"Who was the guy in the car?" I asked. "What did he look like?"

"I don't know." She shrugged. "He had a military haircut, like a buzz cut, and wore sunglasses. He seemed like he was in really good shape, but I'm not sure why I thought that. He stayed in the car. It was just all so secretive that it scared me."

"Any chance you saw a license plate?" I asked.

She shook her head. "I was too far away."

I thought for a minute. "And you have no idea who he is."

She bit her lip, and then made the decision to say what she was thinking. "I don't know if this is true or not, or just some stupid rumor, okay?"

I nodded.

"I've been hearing people in the business talk about a college 'fixer.'" She used her fingers to make quotation marks.

"A fixer?"

"Yeah, like that *Ray Donovan* TV show, but for rich kids trying to get into college," she explained.

Whoa. My dad loved that show with its high drama and Boston accents. On the show, zillionaire Hollywood types paid Ray Donovan loads of money to kill, con, and threaten people.

"How could that be a real job?" I asked. "Who would pay someone to do illegal things to help their kid get into college?"

She looked at me as if I didn't get it. "Rich people pay an absolute *ton* of money—from preschool tuition to college prep—all for their children to be admitted to the 'right' school," she said.

I must have looked like I didn't believe her, because she added, "Look at this school. We're a couple of miles from two amazing public high schools, like tops in the whole freakin' country, but these kids' parents pay thirty thousand dollars a year for the fantasy that it prepares them better than those public schools."

"Thirty thousand a year?" I suddenly had the urge to double my PTA donation.

"Yes," she said. "And every single one of the parents, even if their kid doesn't have good grades and spends all their time playing video games, expects their child to go to Yale."

I was still stuck on the money. "Thirty thousand? Every year?"

"That's what I'm trying to tell you," she said. "It's well-known in the industry that it's worth about *a million and half dollars* to get a kid into an Ivy League school. Someone who can guarantee that will make a heck of a lot of money."

Suddenly, this investigation opened up a lot more avenues. And about a million and a half reasons to commit murder.

* * * *

Quincy called me in the afternoon. "Zoey wants to go ahead with our plan."

"Oh that's great," I said. "When's the first step?"

"Little Red will get his summons tomorrow," he said. "Want to watch it with me?"

"Absolutely!" I said. "But how? He might recognize me if he sees me."

"I'm borrowing my niece's van that she uses for her flower warehouse business," he said. "It's one of those big white vans with no windows and nothing printed on the side."

"Is Zoey coming?" I asked.

He paused. "We agreed that it's better if she doesn't. I promised to send her a video of the whole thing."

"Perfect," I said. "Hey, why are you calling him 'Little Red'?"

"Because he's a bully who hits women a lot smaller than him. He does it because it makes him feel like a big man, but inside he knows he's nothing."

I had avoided thinking too much about the fact that this jerk had actually hurt Zoey. To me she was so tough. She was small and wiry, and far stronger than she looked. She lifted three cases of canned cat food at a time for her job and went to the gym regularly. She also belonged to some kind of martial arts dojo where she'd been steadily moving up in belts.

"Little Red it is."

* * * *

Norma didn't show up for Margarita Night on Wednesday, and I could totally understand why. I'd told her everything, so she had a lot of work to do. I hadn't told her Jaxon's name, and she didn't push for it. She said she'd question Ian about what Jaxon had told me.

Lani was wide-eyed about the idea of a "fixer." "And he drives around giving orders out of his Mercedes?" she asked.

We'd already devoured one bowl of Pico's homemade taco chips when they arrived warm and salty along with the two helpings of salsa we always requested. I picked at the crumbs, a little sad that we had turned down a second serving.

"That's what Ja--, the ex-employee said," I said, struggling not to use her name. "Some kind of luxury car."

"You're not even going to tell me who she is?" She sounded insulted.

I shook my head. "She's really not involved. She just provided information that might not even be relevant."

"Right." Lani pointed the margarita straw at me, dripping on the table before setting it back into the frosted glass. "You've developed an instinct for all this crime stuff. You know it's involved in some way, you just don't know how it all fits together yet."

I rolled my eyes. "I asked the ex-employee if she had any ideas of why someone would want to kill Benson."

"I'm sure she just loved that question," Lani said. "Did she tell you anything?"

"Nope," I said. "She couldn't figure out how or why, just that there's something weird about that company, and maybe he was involved too."

Lani sat back against the leather booth cushions. "We need a meeting to update our suspect list," Lani said. "Do you think Yollie can come over tomorrow? Oh wait. Tomorrow's opening night! Is Elliott excited?"

"He's delirious," I said. "I can't wait to see him, I mean, everyone on stage."

"Piper isn't working, so she gets to be there," Lani said. "Barring an emergency, of course."

I looked up to try to catch Pico's eye for some more chips at the same time that Gemma walked in. She looked around the restaurant, and I was so stunned that I didn't hide in time.

"Oh. My. God," I said. There was only one reason she was here. She saw me across the restaurant and headed my way.

"What?" Lani looked over her shoulder. "Oh. This can't be good," she added as Gemma moved toward us. Every man she passed stared after her as if she had some magic thread that caught them.

"Maybe you should go to the bathroom or something," I told Lani, who surprised me by actually leaving right before Gemma made it to my table. Of course she knew I'd tell her everything anyway.

"Kai said you always come here," Gemma said, looking around as if trying to figure out why.

No way was I telling her about the yummy food and margaritas, or giving her any reason to eat here. "Is everything okay with Joss and Kai?" I asked.

She sneered at me. "Of course it is. That's why I'm here."

"Oh?" I tried to mimic her self-confidence but it came out nasally and unpleasant instead.

She slid into Lani's side of the booth. "I'm here to appeal to your good nature." She batted her eyes at me with a self-righteous expression. "To ask you, for the sake of our family, to step back. To give our family a chance."

"What do you mean?" She was going to have to spell it out.

She gave a little huff. "I want us to be a family again. Look, Joss is too much of a gentleman to make you feel bad by breaking up with you." She leaned toward me, pretending that she felt sorry for me. "You know that our divorce was all me. Once Joss knows I want him back, he'll feel terrible, but he will get rid of you. You could save him that grief."

I laughed, and her face changed to cold anger.

Then I thought more about what she said. "Are you coming to some kind of revelation just because he's dating me?"

"Of course not," she said.

"Then why do you suddenly want him back?" I asked.

"I've, I've just changed is all," she stumbled at first, but then her voice grew stronger. "I see now what I threw away, because life in Alaska was just too hard. Joss understands that it was never about him, it was because I wasn't made to thrive in such a cold place like that."

If I believed her, I might actually consider doing what she suggested, especially if I thought that was what Joss wanted.

"Okay, how's this?" I leaned forward. "We're all grown-ups here." I paused, raising my eyebrows in a "right?" expression. "So, like a grown-up, I'm going to ask Joss what he wants. We'll see what he says and we'll go from there, with no hard feelings. What do you say?"

Her eyes flashed. "Fine. We'll see who he chooses." She slid out of the booth.

I had to admit that when I saw most of the restaurant watch her leave, I had a moment of misgiving. Even scowling, she was beautiful.

Lani must have been watching because she was back in her seat in a flash. I told her what Gemma wanted.

"You have nothing to worry about. I've seen the way Joss looks at you," she said with certainty. "That witch doesn't stand a chance."

Chapter 15

Quincy wanted to make sure he caught Little Red at home, or at his mother's home, so we met early at the kitchen and headed over. We parked about half a block away, with a perfect view of his front yard.

The "process server" knocked on the front door several times, before an older woman opened it. We couldn't hear what they said, but the woman yelled back into the house.

Red came to the door wearing a stretched out T-shirt that may have been white at some point, and long basketball shorts. He looked really angry when he realized what was happening, but then he opened the summons and read it.

He broke into a wide grin and went back inside.

Quincy hit stop on the video app on his phone.

"That went well," I said, as Quincy pulled out and we drove back to work.

"So far, so good," he said. "Maybe this will keep him away from her for a while. She needs a break."

* * * *

Tod dug up some old dirt on Marco Anderson, the HOA president in Benson's neighborhood. It seemed that he hadn't really "retired" from his last job as much as "was fired." He'd been working for a small nonprofit in Los Angeles as part of their fundraising team. He'd been so pushy that potential donors complained to the staff, and the board of directors actually removed him from his post.

I'd never been involved with a nonprofit other than the PTA, but it probably took a lot to be pushed out of that kind of position. It still seemed totally implausible that his zeal to uphold the HOA standards would result in Benson's murder, but I had to meet with him to be sure.

Marco was more than happy to meet me and tell me everything he knew about Benson. We met outside Benson's house and after about ten minutes of listening to Marco list all of his complaints about the property, I realized that he just wanted someone new to vent to.

He was spitting mad that someone had killed Benson and stymied his efforts to have the property made perfect.

"But now someone new will move in," I interrupted, trying to make him feel better and also to stop his ranting.

He waved both hands at the bombed out garage. "Who's going to fix this? The owner lives overseas and takes forever to fix anything!" He pointed to a brown patch in the grass. "Do you know how many times I've cited them for that mess?"

"That mess" was about a foot in diameter at its widest. "How terrible," I said. "What do you know about Benson personally?"

"Basically nothing," he said. "He never participated in any HOA activities. Not the potlucks. Or the pool parties. Or even the Bake-Offs." He was getting even louder. "What kind of sociopath doesn't like Bake-Offs?"

"Hmm." I gave him a sympathetic nod.

"I told everyone, just you wait," he said. "He's going to be some kind of serial killer and we're all going to be standing around saying, 'But he was so quiet.'" He said the last sentence with a sneer.

"Well, at least that didn't happen," I said cheerfully.

"Yeah." He scowled at the house, clearly undecided which was worse.

"So he didn't interact with anyone around here?" I asked, needing any excuse to get away from this Eeyore in human form.

He shook his head. "Not that I know of." Then he snapped his fingers. "Wait. He hired my housekeeper, Fabiola. You should talk to her."

"That'd be great," I said. "Can I have her number?"

"I shoulda thought of her earlier," he said, after reading off her number. "Definitely talk to her. Housekeepers know things."

* * * *

I was still trying to extricate myself from the claws of the one-sided conversation with Marco about how incredible Fabiola was at cooking eggplant parmesan, "just like you're in Florence," and complaining that he couldn't find a good Italian restaurant anywhere close to Sunnyside, when my phone rang. It was Yollie.

"Excuse me!" I was forced to practically yell over his latest harangue and walked toward my car. I waved good-bye, pointing at my phone with an expression of fake regret on my face. "Oh thank goodness," I said to Yollie when I closed the car door.

He watched me leave and I wondered if he was going to file a complaint about my car needing to be washed.

"Can you come to the salon right now?" She spoke in a hushed mumble.

I matched her tone. "Sure, why?"

"That rich girl is here." She hung up.

It took me a while to remember that one of her stylist friends had said something about one of her rich clients and college when we were talking about Benson. Maybe there was a connection I didn't know.

Looks like I was getting my wish to have my copper stripe updated.

I made it to the salon in a few minutes and Yollie was waiting at the receptionist's desk. "Hurry," she said, and led me to a different chair, right beside an eighteen-year-old who was getting her shoulder-length hair dyed an interesting shade that seemed to be somewhere between gray and lavender. She snapped her gum and tapped her fingers on the leather armrests incessantly.

Yollie went to the back to mix my hair dye, and I met the teen's eyes in the mirror. We both smiled awkwardly and looked away.

Her stylist must be in on what I was trying to accomplish because she asked, "How are those college apps going, Bo?"

"All done." She threw both hands in the air as if she'd just made a slam dunk.

"Already?" I gave her an admiring glance in the mirror. "My son's not even close."

She grinned smugly.

"Any suggestions on how I can get him going?" I tried.

"Well, you can remind him that it *is* the rest of his life."

Could she be any more pompous? I forced my smile to stay on my face. "Done that. Any other ideas?"

Her stylist asked, "You should give her the name of the guy that helped you."

Bo lost a bit of her bluster. "I don't actually know the guy," she said.

"What guy?" I asked.

"Tell her," the hairdresser said.

She gave in to the woman who held the fate of her hair color in her hands. And would soon be holding scissors. "My parents dealt with him. I don't have, like, a number or anything."

"What did he do?" I kept my voice friendly with just a little bit of pushiness behind it.

"He helped you with your grades, right?" the stylist said.

"No," she said. "Well, yes."

I wasn't sure where this was going. "Like a tutor?"

"No," Bo said. "He changed grades."

What? "Cool," I said. "I didn't know that was even possible."

Bo's face was beginning to look panicked. "I'm not sure. I don't know how he did it. He just helped my GPA a bit."

Yollie returned and started partitioning my hair into sections.

"That sounds awesome," I said, meeting her eyes in the mirror in between chunks of hair falling in my face. "Can you give my number to your parents and they can give it to him?"

"Sure," she said, relieved that I wasn't asking more uncomfortable questions.

"Wait, here's my card." I pulled it out of my purse.

She shoved it in her pocket without looking at it.

I had a feeling my card wasn't going anywhere but the nearest garbage can, but I'd picked up one more piece of the puzzle. And had someone else for Norma to question.

* * * *

I headed home with a dazzling copper stripe and the wonderful feeling that my hair looked great. On the way, I tried Fabiola, but it went to voice mail. Then I called Jaxon, my new expert in everything college counselor related.

"Hello Colbie." Her voice sounded resigned as if she'd already figured out that I wasn't done with her.

"Thanks so much for taking my call," I said. "I just have one hypothetical question. Is it possible to change the grades in the system that high schools use to send to colleges?"

She thought for a minute. "I hate to say it but it's not *im*possible. It would take a lot of coordination. Like, I have access to the grading system here at the school. But if I changed a grade and it didn't match what the student put in for their grade, then it would raise a red flag. But, if the student was working with me, or their parents were, we could both put in the same grades. Then I'd have to put them back or a teacher here might notice. And I'd have to be really organized because colleges require us to send grades at the end of the semester and a final transcript at the end of the school year. Any differences would be a problem."

"But it could be done," I said. Okay, I had more than one question.

"Yes."

"But only by someone inside the school, like someone in counseling." Someone like a counseling secretary.

"Right."

I swore.

"What?" she asked.

"I have someone to talk to."

* * * *

I tried to tell myself that just because it was possible, didn't mean it happened. And even if it happened, like Bo said, that didn't mean that Opal was guilty of changing grades.

But my instincts were telling me this was an important piece of the puzzle. Unfortunately, I knew that Opal wouldn't let me anywhere near her.

I called Norma and told her my latest suspicions. That maybe Benson and Opal worked together to help kids get into college. Benson wrote the recommendation letters and Opal changed the grades. All for money.

"Interesting theory," she said. "I'll add that to my list to ask her when she comes back from vacation."

"What?" It seemed like a really bad time for her to be on vacation. Wasn't she supposed to be helping students with their college apps?

"She sent an email yesterday saying she had to go home for a family emergency and was taking vacation to cover it."

"That was the day after I talked to her," I said.

Norma was quiet for so long that I worried she was mad at me for talking to Opal. Then she nodded. "I guess I better try harder to find her."

Chapter 16

I put the whole Benson mess to the side in time to pick up Elliott from the middle school and drive him and a few friends over to the high school. They were all so excited they were practically jumping in their seats. "I can't wait until the audience sees us come in!" said someone from the back seat.

Elliott turned around with wide eyes. "They are gonna sh—. Go crazy."

The boys laughed loudly at his almost slipup.

I gasped, pretending to be offended. "I have no idea where he learned such language."

"Right," Elliott said.

I drove behind the school to the loading dock for the theater and saw Tuesday, the puppet inspecting lady, unloading her minivan. "Boys, help her out."

They all crowded around happy to help by puppeteering the puppets into the prop area. I wheeled a rack of costumes down the ramp of the rental truck and up the loading dock, delighted to have some small part in the production. I usually got much more involved in Elliott's theater projects but I'd held back from committing to any volunteer work during the last few months. Gearing my business up to put my products on the shelves of Twomey's stores had taken all of my time.

My phone rang with an unknown number and I answered. "Hello?"

A woman's voice with a slight accent said, "Hello, this is Fabiola."

I walked away from the crowd of middle school students. "Thank you for calling me back. I was hoping to talk to you about what you knew about Benson Tadworth."

"All I did was clean his house," she said. "I don't know anything about him, really."

"Marco mentioned that since you cleaned for him, you might know something that he, I don't know, kept secret. Even from his friends." She was silent for so long that I thought we'd been cut off. "Hello?" I asked.

"He had a hiding place," she said. "I saw him take money out of it, by accident, once. It's under the floorboards in the dining room."

"Yes, the police found that," I said, disappointed. "Anything else?"

"No," she said. "That's all. But I still have the key. Should I give it to someone?"

* * * *

No way was I going to mess with Norma's crime scene by getting the key from her and exploring the inside of Benson's house, no matter how much I wanted to. Instead, I called Norma and gave her Fabiola's phone number. I had a play to get ready for.

After I told Elliott and his friends to "break a leg," they all headed backstage to join the rest of the cast to wait for the pizza to be delivered. My dad, Annie, Lani, Piper, Joss, Kai, and I ate at Pico's. Pico said he had tickets for the Saturday matinee, and added, "And I hope my sons don't burn the place down while I'm gone," he yelled over his shoulder.

One of his sons rolled his eyes as he delivered a plate of plantains to Kai for dessert.

Then we headed over to the florist, picking up far too many bouquets for Elliott, and drove over to the high school with plenty of time to get our seats.

Middle school friends of the drama club had put down a red carpet and acted like paparazzi for the family members and friends arriving for the first night of *The Lion King*.

Richard joined us, sliding his flowers for Elliott under his seat and shaking hands with everyone. Norma and her daughter slid into their seats minutes before the middle school band warmed up and the curtain rose.

From the moment the first note soared out over the audience, to the gasps from the audience when they saw the parade of crazy-colored animals winding its way down the aisles, to the last chorus of young voices coming together for the rousing "Hakuna Matata" song before intermission, I was transfixed. When Elliott ran out on stage as Zazu, I grabbed my dad's hand hard and tears came to my eyes. It happened at every one of his shows. Elliott was so happy to be on stage.

Richard came over to me in the lobby during intermission when Joss and Kai left to buy a drink. "I should probably tell you something," he said. "You made a big ol' donation to the drama club to help pay for all this," I said.

"Yeah," he said sheepishly. "Elliott already gave me a hard time."

"He did?" I asked. I'd decided to stay out of it, as Lani had suggested. Richard shoved his hands in his pockets and rocked back on his heels. "He's worried that he'll get roles because of the money, so he asked me not to do it anymore."

Wow. I was worried about the perception, and Elliott was worried about it actually happening, that he'd get a role he didn't deserve because of it. I knew he could do anything, so if he got a role, then he earned it.

"He's a great kid, isn't he?" Richard said.

"He's pretty amazing up there on stage," I said.

"Which one is the girl he likes?" he asked.

I blinked. "He told you he likes her?" I asked.

"Yeah." He laughed. "He was asking for advice."

A sharp pain hit me in my chest and I turned away. "She's on the crew so you won't see her on stage." My voice was tight but he didn't seem to notice, busy watching the other parents in the lobby.

Norma came over while her daughter was talking to a friend, and Richard excused himself.

"Anything new?" I asked and immediately wished I hadn't. It would be nice to have a murder-free evening.

She shook her head. "Still trying to track down Opal."

The bell sounded for everyone to take their seats. The second half was as much fun as the first, even when the joints of one of the zebra costumes locked up, and the actor couldn't get it to "run" across the stage.

The sound of the actors' voices singing "The Circle of Life" sent chills down my spine, making me believe for a moment that all was good in the world. They were having so much fun providing their friends and family with this entertainment. Most of them wouldn't go on to a life in theater, but they'd have these memories of fun and friendship working together for a common goal, to create something beautiful.

The African sun rose on stage, as Simba and Nala slowly climbed up Pride Rock and the animals bowed all together. Then Elliott made the Zazu puppet fly around the stage and the animals hailed their new king.

When the final note rang out, the audience came to its feet in a standing ovation, clapping and cheering and woo-hooing as the student actors took their bows with delighted smiles on their shining faces.

The middle school drama club's tradition was to have the actors come out to the lobby in costume to talk to the children in the audience, but the most complex costumes stayed in the back.

Elliott had the Zazu puppet talking to a little girl when we reached him. "I'm glad that you enjoyed it," he said in the parrot's voice. "And now I have to return to the kingdom."

She laughed and ran back to her family.

"I'll be right back," he told us after quick one-armed hugs.

We waited for him, watching the other actors greet their families and friends.

Piper pointed to an antelope with daisy spots. "You really outdid yourself with those costumes," she said to Lani. "The giraffes were my favorite."

Simba's mom interrupted us to tell me what a great job Elliott did.

"You have a star there," I told her.

Norma's phone buzzed and her face changed when she read the screen. "Wonderful show," she said, but her smile was strained. "I have to go."

* * * *

Elliott had a hard time calming down after the show, but eventually he got ready for bed. I went in to say good night, followed by Trouble. He sat up to pet her when she jumped on the bed. "Mom?"

"Yes?" I held my breath.

"Can I ask you a question?" He watched Trouble circle around to arrange herself for sleeping.

"Anytime, kiddo."

He paused for a moment and my heart hurt that he'd changed his mind. Then he spoke really fast, as if trying to get the words out before his brain told him not to. "How do you know if a girl likes you?" He kept his head down but his eyes flicked up to meet mine.

I sat down, smoothing out the Minecraft comforter. "That's a very hard question, even for me, a girl." I smiled. "But for most people, it's pretty clear. It's usually a good sign if she hangs out with you, and sits close to you when she has a chance, and laughs at your jokes, even when they're stupid."

He rolled his eyes. "That's all friend stuff," he said. "How do you know if she *likes* you, likes you?"

"The only way to be sure is to tell her that you *like* her like her and ask if she *likes* you likes you back," I said, hoping for the sake of his special heart that it was true.

He looked unsure.

"Are you talking about Sasha?" I asked.

He nodded.

"Well, from my point of view, you know, because I'm your totally unbiased mother, I think she does like you. But then, I also think she'd be crazy not to."

"Right," he said. "Her mom works backstage a lot and she seems to like me."

"That's also a good sign," I said.

Trouble lifted her head. *Scratch behind her ears and she'll love you forever.*

"She seems like a very nice, very smart girl who won't hate you if I'm wrong," I said. "Just go for it. Ask her."

"Dad told me to buy her a gift." He said it as if he wasn't sure if it was good advice.

"Hmm," I said. "That's a thought. But it's still not answering your question. A friend can buy another friend a present, right?"

He nodded and then gave a deep sigh. First love was always the hardest.

"It'll be okay," I said.

He held out his pinky. "Pinky swear?"

I grabbed his pinky with mine. "Pinky swear." *Please be true.*

He slid down and pulled the covers around his shoulders.

"You know, I just had a thought," I said. "You may want to wait until after the play is over. Because either way, that could be awkward."

He blew out a breath. "Thanks, Mom."

"Anytime," I said. "I'm a wealth of information about girls. And cat food. But not much else."

He snorted and reached over to give me a hug.

I held on extra tight before letting go.

* * * *

Quincy called the next morning when I was sitting at the kitchen table, my head in my hands. The first cup of coffee didn't do its job, and the coffee pot seemed too far away. I should've left it on the table. Or poured cream in it and used it for my mug.

"Good morning, Quincy," I said.

"Are you sick?" he asked. "You sound awful."

"Just tired. Opening night went late," was all I said. I'd spent a couple of hours wondering if I'd given Elliott bad advice. What if I was completely wrong and Sasha never spoke to him again? What if he blamed me? Did I need to talk to him about consent? He was only twelve but what if he decided to do something stupid like kiss her, and she protested, and he got kicked out of school? My thoughts had chased themselves until I fell into a troubled sleep.

"How did it go?" he asked. "Was Elliott incredible as usual?"

"He did great." The memory made me smile again. "He just loves all that, you know?"

"We have tickets for tonight," he said. "Can't wait. But I called about something else."

Oh man. "Something else good or bad?" I asked.

"Good. Really good news," he said. "Norma called. My yogi is finally able to speak, and he verified everything I told the police."

"That's awesome!" I said. Even though I knew the truth would come out, I felt a wave of relief.

I covered the phone and scowled over at Trouble. "I wait on you all the time. You should get me coffee once in a while."

She licked a paw. *Impossible. No opposable thumbs.*

Quincy went on. "Norma said they're releasing a statement this morning. This afternoon, I'm going to call Natural-LA Grocers and tell them they have two weeks to make the decision, or you're going to send the proposal to their primary competitor."

"Really?" I asked. "What if that makes them mad?"

"I think giving them a deadline is the right move," he said. "But it's totally up to you."

He went on about a new marketing plan. "I have at least one reality show celebrity who's willing to wear that T-shirt in front of the paparazzi."

"The one with my logo that says 'My cat eats better than I do'?" I asked with a laugh. His social media person came up with fun ideas like that all the time.

"Yes," he said. "It's catchy and the cameras will eat it up. She's going to carry some of your food into her apartment. When the photos hit, we'll blast them on Twitter."

It was wonderful to have the real Quincy back.

"Okay," I said. "Go ahead with your power move." I bit my lip. At least I'd know their response sooner.

"Hey, maybe you should take a day off," he suggested. "When was the last time you didn't think about Meowio at all?"

"I can't remember," I said with a laugh.

"I'm only saying it because I took it easy this week and today I feel great," he said.

That might have something to do with no longer being a murder suspect.

"You know, we should have a talk sometime about balance," he added.

"We'll see," I said. "I'm going into the kitchen later since the whole drama club has an excused first period only, so I'm letting Elliott sleep in."

"Maybe you should go back to bed for a bit," he suggested. "Anyway, I just wanted you to know that we're back on track."

I could imagine him rubbing his hands together in anticipation.

"And the other matter you helped me with the other day?" he said. "I can show you the progress when you get here."

Ooh. He was talking in code about Little Red. "Can't wait," I said. "Hey, what are you going to do about that DA who had it in for you?"

"Oh he'll get his," Quincy said with a smile in his voice. "The next election will end much differently."

When I got off the phone I saw a text from Jaxon, saying she had more information. I called her right away.

"I've been thinking about A&D and realized some other…stuff," she said.

"Thanks so much for reaching out," I said. People didn't often follow up with me. I usually had to track them down and harass them until they gave in.

"Well, it seems like you're someone who will, I don't know, take action," she said.

"I will," I said.

"The first thing is the president, Ian, used cash *a lot*," she said. "Normal people just don't do that anymore. When he took us out to celebrate something, which believe me didn't happen very often, he always paid cash. And the bookkeeper once told me that he even paid some of the company bills in cash."

Norma had found hidden cash in Benson's house and Fabiola had also seen it. "That's weird."

"And I don't think I made it clear how nervous Ian got when this guy came around, like flop sweat nervous. One time a big BMW revved his engine near us, just like on the street, and I thought he was going to have a heart attack. He jumped back like the guy was going to shoot us or something."

I held my breath. "What happened?"

"It was just some random car," she said. "It drove away."

She seemed like she had more. "Anything else strange?"

"Yeah, he always scanned the parking lot on his way out. It's like he had PTSD and had to be on alert all the time."

Did this mean the fixer was real? And Ian Luther was afraid of him? How could I find out for sure?

I thought about the We Hate Benson Tadworth Facebook group. "Is there some kind of Facebook group for college counselors? If so, I want to see if anyone would be willing to talk to me about this fixer guy."

She thought for a minute. "Not any group that I know of, but there's a monthly networking mixer at a restaurant down in the Gaslamp district. Give me your email address and I'll send you the website. You can sign up there."

"So is this fixer guy the reason you left?" I asked.

She was quiet.

"Jaxon?"

"I hate to admit it, but no." She paused. "I couldn't take the pressure," she said. "I mean, I have plenty of stressed out teens and parents here, but it was so over-the-top there. The students were either demanding little brats or shaking with anxiety. We had these impossible quotas for the number of students that we helped, their SAT score improvements, and the schools they were admitted to. It was too much."

"That sounds awful," I said.

"The parents were the worst. When the Ivy Leagues sent out their admissions, I thought the place would implode."

She paused and said it so quietly I almost didn't hear her. "One of the students tried to commit suicide."

"Oh no," I said.

"I quit the next day."

Chapter 17

I was certainly awake after Jaxon's phone call. I couldn't stop thinking about those poor kids with so much pressure on them to get into the right college. I vowed not to do that to Elliott. Seeing as he had zero interest in anything but musical theater, I was probably safe.

Then I thought about how hard it was to get into a good musical theater program. Maybe we weren't so safe.

I checked out the website Jaxon sent and signed up for the networking event, paying to attend. I received a cheerful automatic email welcoming me to the event and letting me know that my forty-five dollars included appetizers, two drinks and the chance to listen to a speaker discussing the latest ways to help students take the SAT.

Forty-five dollars was definitely worth finding out if the fixer even existed.

* * * *

I had just dropped a drooping Elliott off at school, to join all of the other probably drooping drama club kids, when Yollie called to report on what Steven heard on his recorder. "Well, we can't hear much of anything, but you were right. Steven did forget to turn off his recorder at the end of his lesson. It runs for like five minutes afterwards. Benson is definitely talking to someone, but it's muffled and far away."

I was so excited that it took me a moment to process. "That's great!" I said. "Can I pick it up? Wait. I'm going to call Norma. She'll have her tech guys work on it. They might be able to hear all kinds of things."

"Um, okay," Yollie said, not understanding my enthusiasm.

"Why only five minutes?" I asked, even as I wondered if there was any way to enhance the recording. Didn't they do that all the time on TV police shows?

"Steven thinks that the girl who had the next lesson saw that the recorder was on—she probably saw the red light—and turned it off."

"That makes sense," I said. "Norma will probably send someone over right away to get the recorder."

Yollie sighed. "Fine. But he needs it back fast. He uses that thing every day."

"I'll let her know that," I said. Not that it would help.

Norma answered the phone and seemed as interested in the recording as I was. "Did you hear from Quincy?" she asked.

"Oh yeah," I said. "First thing this morning. That's really good." Then I remembered that she'd been upset after the play. "Is everything okay with you? You looked like you got bad news last night."

She didn't say anything for a while and I waited for her to decide whether to tell me. "Opal Volker isn't with any of her family members. And she hasn't used her phone or credit cards for a couple of days."

"Whoa," I said. "Is she on the run or...?"

"We don't know," she said. "Either of those is bad."

I heard someone call her name through the phone.

"Gotta go." She hung up.

I worried about Opal for a while. She could have taken a vacation and used the family emergency as an excuse. Or maybe she really had been taking money for changing grades and because of my questions, she assumed the police were closing in. Maybe she cashed out so she could start over somewhere. I couldn't help but wonder if there really was a fixer and he'd "fixed" her.

I took a few deep breaths. Then I called Yollie back to let her know an officer was on the way to get the recorder.

"Hey Colbie?" Yollie asked, her voice tentative. "I want to let you know that I feel terrible about the five star review I gave Benson."

"Okay," I said.

"It's really not okay," she said. "I was thinking only about Steven, and trying to save money so I could afford for him to keep going. It was selfish."

"It's over, Yollie," I said. "No need to feel guilty now."

"I'm not so sure," she said. "I can't stop thinking that maybe I ruined someone else's kid. That he or she was abused by Benson and decided against being a musician. All because of my review."

* * * *

I tried to make Yollie feel better but wasn't sure I succeeded. When I was almost at the kitchen, my dad called. "Get back here," he sounded nervous. "A man came to the door. He said your friend Tod sent him."

"Don't let him in," I said. "Tod didn't tell me anything." I made a U-turn and started driving faster.

"I didn't," he said. "He's got some weird equipment and he said he'd get started in the garage."

Oh man. Tod went ahead with having my house checked for bugs? I called him and he picked up.

"Did you send someone to my house?" I asked.

"Yes, he's checking for electronic surveillance," Tod said. "I told you it was important."

"You could have given me a head's up," I said, sounding cranky.

"This way it's harder for you to say no," he said.

"Fine."

I hung up and called my dad back. "You can let him in," I said. "I didn't tell you before but Tod thinks we should have the house checked for bugs because we found the GPS tracker."

"Great," my dad said sarcastically. "It's like having Jason Bourne living here."

"Hey!" I protested.

"I'm sorry," he said. "If it'll help you be safe, let's do it."

"I'll be home soon."

* * * *

Tod's friend wouldn't tell me his name when I introduced myself. I gestured to his shirt, which had the word "Wizard" emblazoned diagonally across it. "I have to call you something. How about Wizard?"

"Sure," he said.

Twenty minutes later he was pointing a weird piece of electronics, which looked like a Star Trek tricorder, at my dining room chandelier. He put a finger to his mouth. Then he pulled a wire from inside the chandelier, so small that I'd never noticed it before. At the end of it was a tiny microphone.

Trouble sat staring at it, as if to say, *Finally*. She'd been watching the chandelier for days. Could she sense the bug?

My heart started pounding. I gestured with my hand for him to pull it out and he shook his head. Then he continued around the house, finding another one in the kitchen under a cabinet and one in my dad's office, attached to his small desk fan. The family room caused some issues because of the television, but he ultimately said it was fine, as well as all of the rooms upstairs.

"I'm calling the police," I whispered.

He shook his head and whispered back. "Not yet." He held out his hand. "Your phone?"

My phone? My hands shook as I put in the password and handed it to him. I made sure he couldn't see what I typed, but I got the impression he could figure it out if he wanted. He spent a few minutes looking at my phone, clicking around to different apps on the home screen. "It's clean," he said.

I went into the living room and dialed Norma. This investigation was getting odder every day.

* * * *

Of course, Norma had to see them for herself. "What the actual hell?" she said quietly, when I pointed to the bug in the dining room. Wizard had made sure to be gone when she got there, but I assumed Tod could reach him if he was needed.

Norma had brought along a crime scene investigator who treated them as evidence, which of course they were. He placed numbers by them, took a million photos, and then ripped them out and put them in plastic evidence bags.

We stayed quiet until the last one was packed away and then Norma and I sat down in the now bug-free dining room. "You ever been bugged?" I asked her.

She shook her head. "Not as far as I know."

"It's a creepy feeling," I said. "I keep wondering what I've talked about around them, what my dad has talked about—" My voice hitched. "Elliott."

Norma grabbed my hand. "We'll get him," she said.

I nodded, and tried to push back the anxiety that was pressing against the back of my throat, like a scream that wanted to come out. Then I took a deep breath, and told her the latest from Jaxon. Again, without telling her who was giving me the information.

"You know, this BMW has come up a few times," I said. "I saw a black BMW at Benson's and Jaxon mentioned the scary dude drove a luxury car. She said a Mercedes but maybe it was really a BMW."

"Could be," she said. "There's too many of them here. I can't do much with it until we get more." She seemed frustrated, like she felt that was important too. "Supposedly, the president of A&D, that Ian Luther, really is on vacation. And no one there is authorized to talk to us."

"Could you hear anything on Steven's tape?" I asked.

She nodded. "We have a man's voice saying Benson was making a mistake. It sounded threatening but the DA said even if we find the guy, it's not enough. We have to prove he actually did something."

My dad came into the dining room. "I gotta lunch date with Annie." He looked at the chandelier and shook his head. "You gotta get a new hobby," he said.

* * * *

The second performance of *The Lion King* was even better than the first, but I was having a hard time enjoying it. Gemma had brought Kai.

"Surprise!" Kai ran up to Joss and me while we waited in line to get in. She hopped up and down in excitement. "My mom said we could come! I get to see Elliott be Zazu again!"

Then Gemma joined us, smiling and looking gorgeous. Whatever she did to her eyes was magical.

Joss introduced us again, seeming to forget we'd already met at my house.

"That's nice of you to bring Kai again," I said.

"Oh she loves these things," she said. "I couldn't let her miss it."

Gemma and Kai were in the row behind us, and I spent the whole first act forcing myself not to turn around and see if she was watching us, especially when Joss put his arm along the back of my seat.

Luckily, Quincy was also there, giving me a buffer during intermission. He'd brought his extended family, including eight grandchildren. The adults were in a celebratory mood and kept telling me how very impressed they were with the young actors. The grandchildren were entranced by the animal puppets, of course.

"You missed seeing the video of the progress," he said.

"What happened?" I asked. "Did Red fall for it?"

"Hook, line and sinker." He looked around and pulled out his phone, clicking on a link. "Here he is going into the lab. And here he is in the waiting room."

I squinted. "It looks so real."

"QP Diagnostics at your service," he said.

"You can see it another time with the sound on," he said. "The man said some vulgar things about DNA samples."

"Ugh," I said. "I don't need to hear that."

We could see the receptionist check his driver's license and then take a very official-looking DNA kit out of a metal cabinet. She swabbed the inside of Red's cheek, carefully putting the oversized Q-tip back in the bag, sealing it, and giving Red a receipt. "What's that?"

"It has the same number as on the bag, so he can make sure he got the correct paperwork when his results show up," Quincy explained.

We watched him saunter out of the lab, with an expression on his face indicating that everything was going his way.

"Oh man," I said. "It'll be nice for Zoey to have him out of her life, forever."

I decided not to tell Quincy about the bugs. He didn't need something else to worry about, and this definitely wasn't the time or place.

Chapter 18

The next day, Elliott and I stopped by Chubby's Pizza to pick up the lunch order for the cast. I'd skipped the farmers' market so I could see the Saturday matinee performance, and also pitch in to help a bit.

While we were waiting for the last couple of pizzas to be boxed up, my nutritional pyramid scheme buddy came in. He immediately looked guilty and wished he could turn around and leave.

"Oh sorry I didn't get to the farmers' market again," he said.

"That's okay." I laughed. "I'm not there today either." I introduced him to Elliott. "Drake, right?"

They shook hands.

"Drake bought some Meowio food for his cat," I told Elliott.

"Yeah," Drake said, sounding apologetic. "Digger liked it, but, you know."

I'd run into this many times. People had their cat try my food and either the cat didn't like it, which was rare, or the owner didn't want to pay more for their cat's food. Then they were embarrassed to talk to me.

"No problem," I said. "You are under no obligation to buy my products."

He still looked sheepish. "Thanks for being so kind. Hey, you guys want to eat here instead of takeout? My treat."

"No," I said. "But thank you." The cashier arrived with the first six boxes. "Taking these to a bunch of hungry kids."

"Have fun," he said. "Maybe I'll see you at the ol' Chubb-meister again sometime."

"Chubb-meister?" Elliott said, once we were out of earshot.

I laughed. "He's the pushy salesman type. They have their own lingo."

We loaded up the car with the help of the cashier and I drove slowly to the high school. The drama kids attacked the pizzas, eating more than

I thought possible. Then it was a rush to clean everything up, including faces and hands, before putting the costumes on and taking to the stage.

Norma sent me a text. *When you're done with the show, can I stop by so you can listen to Steven's recording?*

I texted back. *Sure, but I'm stuck here until after tonight's show. Want to stop by during the dinner break?*

That works, she texted back. *I'll bring sandwiches.*

* * * *

Norma came through, bringing overstuffed sandwiches from Load It Up Subs on Main Street, turkey for me and roast beef for her. As always, I assumed that I'd never be able to eat that much food and less than half an hour later, the whole delicious thing was gone.

We sat in her car, the steady rain making me feel like we were cut off from the rest of the world. She played an enhanced version of the recording. Some of it was still muffled, but plenty of it was clear.

"What do you want?" Benson said. "I have a student waiting."

"… change your mind."

I looked up at Norma and she shook her head, indicating that something was still missing.

"Look, I have to do it. My reputation is taking a beating. All he had to do was stick to our agreement." Benson's voice sounded resentful but determined.

The next sound was just a murmur.

"It is a big deal!" Benson said. "Look, I'm pulling it and you can't do anything about it. You shouldn't even be here."

The response was clear. "We'll see about that." The tone was definitely menacing.

"Yikes," I whispered.

"Look, I'll give you the money back."

The answer was muffled but something along the lines of not wanting the money back, and then more of something I couldn't make out.

Benson said loudly, "Don't threaten me." Then, a door slammed.

Norma turned off the recording. "The next student came in, saw that the recorder was still running, and turned it off. She also overheard the tone of the argument but couldn't make out any words. And Benson was sweaty and angry during her lesson, and apparently, 'even meaner' than normal."

"That's great," I said. "All you have to do is match the voice with a suspect and you have him."

"That's not necessarily true," she said. "We have proof that he was threatening Benson, but that's not enough."

"But it matches up to the rumors Tabitha, the other oboe teacher, heard. That Benson was paid for a good recommendation and that the student went back on their deal. It sounds like Benson was going to do something about it."

"Do you recognize the voice?" Norma asked.

I thought about it and shook my head. "There's a certain quality, I guess that is the best way to describe it, that sounds familiar. But I can't place it at all."

Her expression didn't change. "We're sending the recording off to the FBI. They have better equipment. We'll see what they can capture."

"Did you find out anything about the bugs?" I asked, the word still making me shiver.

Norma shook her head. "Same as the GPS tracker. Military grade equipment but nothing traceable."

She looked over my shoulder at the same time someone knocked on the door. I jumped and turned, almost dropping my soda and making Norma laugh.

"Mom?" Elliott asked. "What are you doing out here?" He was wearing his hood up over his head to protect himself from the rain. "You're on backstage duty."

I opened the window an inch. "I'll be in soon."

He frowned and went back to the theater.

"Does he know about all this?" Norma asked.

"No," I said. "I'll figure out what to tell him when his show is over."

* * * *

Trouble's snarling announced that Charlie the chicken had come to visit, right before the "Yankee Doodle Dandy" doorbell rang. Luckily my dad was already sitting at the kitchen table drinking his coffee and reading the Sunday paper, and Elliott was sleeping so hard, nothing could wake him up.

Charlie was alone this time and I walked him back to the farm, skirting the puddles that remained from last night's rain.

My dad's neighbor, Horace, waved from his front porch. "Good morning," he called out. He was holding a glass that I knew was filled with iced tea sweetened with as much sugar as a bowl of Fruit Loops.

Charlie heard him and took a detour, heading straight for Horace's doorbell. Unfortunately, there wasn't a conveniently placed planter to hop on and get up to it. Charlie tilted his head back and forth, feathers drooping into his eyes, and then gave up.

Horace shook his head. "He does the same thing every time." He leaned over to scratch Charlie's head and added affectionately, "Bird brain." Then he looked up at me. "You going to see those baby goats?"

"Yep," I said. "They're the cutest."

"Maybe I can go with you," he said.

"Sure." I helped him up out of his wooden rocking chair, and he held onto my arm walking down the steps.

Horace had once been almost six feet tall but age had shrunken him to my height. He always wore a tank top with overalls, even when it was chilly, claiming that the weather didn't affect him much.

"How are things going with your fella'?" he asked as we slowly made our way the rest of the block to the farm.

"Doing good," I said.

"You sure?" he asked.

What did that mean? "I think so, why?"

"That ex-wife of his bin showin' her face." He sounded like he didn't want to gossip but wanted to warn me. "She's there now."

I stopped still. "Like, arrived this morning? Or...?"

He nodded. "Bright and early this morning. Then the next thing I see is that chicken running down the road."

It took me a few steps to realize what he was hinting at. "Wait. Do you think Gemma set Charlie loose so he'd go get me? On purpose?"

He shrugged with a *don't ask me* expression.

We resumed walking. "Interesting," I said. "Let's see what she's up to."

Sure enough, when we arrived, Gemma was standing next to Joss. As we got closer, I could see that she was showing him photos on her camera, and then she full-on leaned her body against his. I put Charlie back in his pen, noting that the gate was open, so I closed it. I guess Gemma didn't know that Charlie didn't need an open gate to escape.

Joss moved to the side, away from Gemma. She actually looked over her shoulder to make sure I was there and threw her arms around his neck.

"Well, isn't this a nice spectacle?" Horace murmured.

Even though I knew the whole scene was directed toward me, like some kind of soap opera, I had to subdue my knee-jerk reaction to pull her arms off of Joss's neck and maybe off of her body. And then I had to subdue my second knee-jerk reaction, which was to turn around and escape without seeing Joss's reaction.

Horace must have sensed something because he put his hand on my arm to keep me beside him.

Joss took a step back, pulled on Gemma's arms and said something like, "What the hell are you doing?" She'd made sure his back was to us and so far, he hadn't seen us.

She still clung to him like a limpet for a moment before letting go. Then she covered her face with her hands and her shoulders heaved. She tried to move closer for him to hold her, and instead, he grabbed her by the shoulders with his elbows locked to keep her as far away from him as possible.

"Show's over folks," Horace said.

* * * *

"You did what?" Lani demanded when I told her the story.

"I walked with Horace back to his porch and went home," I said, feeling proud of myself.

"Did you see her drive away at least?" she asked. "She had to pass by your house to get out of there, right?"

"Oh yes," I said. "I took a cup of coffee out to the front porch, and when she drove by, I raised it to her."

"Ooh," she said. "Like 'screw you' or like 'you're a worthy adversary'?"

I laughed. "Probably a combination of both."

"Are you going to tell Joss you saw the whole thing?" She sounded delighted with how things turned out.

"No!" I said.

"Hmm," she said. "I bet he tells you."

I hoped Joss would, but he hadn't contacted me at all by the time we left for the Sunday matinee performance of *The Lion King*. Elliott was sad that it was the last performance, but the drama club teacher sponsor had encouraged them to think about ideas for their spring show.

"Maybe they can do *Hairpray* in the spring," my dad suggested. "Didn't you push for that one?"

"I don't know," Elliott said. "Not as many kids were as excited about it as I was."

"Well, one of those reasons was because Lani designed the costumes for *The Lion King*," I said. "Why don't you see what she can do for that musical?"

"Hmm," he said, thinking for a bit. "Or," he drew out the word, "we can think about another musical where Lani can go wild."

"Like what?"

"What about *The Little Mermaid*?" he said, getting excited. "Can you imagine what Lani would do with that?" He pulled out his phone.

"Are you texting Lani?" I asked.

"No," he said. "Sasha." He frowned at me. "Don't. Say. Anything."

My dad was very careful to look out his window to hide his grin.

* * * *

As usual, the last show was over far too quickly. I wished I could bottle up all of that innocent fun on stage, especially the way it made me feel. My dad wasn't interested in staying for the cast party, so he got a ride home.

Some of the actors cried at the party, already missing their brief but intense time together.

Elliott and Sasha sat together the whole time. I thought I saw them holding hands, but when I tried to slide over to get a better angle, Tuesday the puppet inspector was in my way.

"Elliott did a remarkable job," she said.

"Thank you." I tried to keep my eyes on her face, but they kept drifting over to the potential lovebirds near the piano.

She peered at me over her glasses. "Do you think he'd be interested in getting additional training? We have puppetry classes at the guild starting soon."

That surprised me. "I don't know," I said. "He probably doesn't know they exist."

"Is it okay if I invite him to take the classes?" she asked. "I like to get parents' permission before I ask."

"Of course," I said.

Elliott and Sasha moved apart when Tuesday approached.

Shoot. Now I couldn't see anything. Elliott smiled when they spoke, but I couldn't tell if he was humoring her or genuinely interested in puppetry classes.

I wondered what my dad would think of that. He'd just recently embraced the whole musical theater hobby of Elliott's once he figured out that it was okay that his grandson had no interest in playing football. Puppetry might be a step too far.

* * * *

Elliott was quiet on the way home, but he kept smiling when he looked out the window.

"Everything okay?" I asked.

He nodded but didn't say anything.

I couldn't take the suspense anymore and went for it. "So," I drew out the word, "it seems as if she *likes* you likes you."

A grin spread on his face. "I think so."

I breathed a sigh of relief. "Anything you want to add?"

"No, Mom," he said. "It's private."

Really? I'd get more out of him later. "What do you think about taking puppetry classes?" I asked.

He shrugged. "They seem like fun, but they're downtown on Saturdays during the farmers' market."

"Don't worry about that," I said. "We'll figure it out."

"Maybe I'll try one?" he said. "But I don't know. I liked it but it's not the kind of theater I want to do."

My dad had brought more Pico's burritos home and we heated them up for a quick dinner. Afterward, Elliott went up to his room to finish his homework. His junior theater performances always messed with his school schedule but he usually had understanding teachers who let him make up his work.

I wasn't entirely surprised to answer the door and see Joss on the porch, looking agitated. "I have to tell you something and I don't want you to be upset." His hair was tousled, like he'd been running his hands through it.

"Okay," I said. I joined him outside and closed the door behind us.

Trouble jumped up on her windowsill perch, watching intently. *You better watch it, mister.*

"You were right." He shook his head like he couldn't believe it. "Gemma said she wants me back. That she wants us to be a family again."

I held my breath.

"I told her there wasn't a chance in hell," he said.

"Okay," I said. "You don't look happy about that."

"I'm fine," he said. "Really. But I'm worried that she'll do something to retaliate. Like challenge Kai's custody again."

Oh man. I hadn't thought about what she could do to mess with their lives. "You have an agreement," I said. "You'd just have to take her to court. And Kai's old enough now that the judge would take her feelings into account, right?"

"Right," he said. "Logically, I know that's all true. But I can't trust her because of what she pulled this summer."

"It'll be okay," I said.

"But I came over here for another reason," he said. "I know it's just about the worst possible timing, but I have to get it out."

He grabbed both of my hands. My heart started pounding at the look in his eyes. "Okay."

My phone rang from my back pocket.

No! I could've screamed.

Joss looked as frustrated as I felt.

"Ignore it," I said, wanting to throw it far away. "I'll turn it off." I fumbled with it to send the call to voice mail and we both saw that it was Norma calling. "Shoot."

"Go ahead and take it," he said. "This can wait."

"Hi, Norma," I said, striving to sound calm.

"I have some bad news," she said.

"What?" A slew of possible bad news scenarios went through my brain.

"We found Opal Volker," she said.

I could tell it from her voice. "She's dead, isn't she?"

Chapter 19

Joss never did tell me what he had to "get out." I guess talking about dead bodies puts the kibosh on any other conversation.

Norma had spared me most of the horrible details about Opal's death but what she did tell me was awful. Her body had been found in the middle of El Monte Park, a county park of hiking trails through mountains and valleys, east of Sunnyside. The only reason she was discovered was because someone saw a coyote with clothing in its mouth and tracked him back to Opal.

I stopped Norma from saying any more at that point.

Opal had never been on vacation. She'd been dead since Tuesday night or early Wednesday morning. The coroner wasn't yet able to narrow it down more than that.

A part of me had suspected the worst ever since I heard she'd taken an emergency vacation but having it confirmed was awful. Now Norma was investigating who had access to her email and could've written the message that she was leaving town.

"You need to be careful," she said. "We have no suspects. We tracked down Ian Luther but he's not talking. I'm going to flash a few photos of her body to get him to open up."

Norma didn't pull any punches when she had two homicides to solve.

* * * *

Quincy and I were in place outside Red's house when the same process server showed up to give Red the results of his DNA test. He was waxing his car and greeted the server with a grin. Since his hands were dirty from the wax, he told him to put the envelope in his mouth.

"Gross," I said.

The server left in a hurry, which was a very smart thing to do.

Red wiped his hands on the rag sticking out of his back pocket, and opened the envelope. He read the results, and even from a distance, we could see his face turning red and then purple with rage.

Quincy zoomed in the video camera to catch Red screaming at the sky like a wild beast. He ripped up the papers, grasping at the pieces with two hands, and throwing them away from him. Then he picked up a tool from the ground and held it like a baseball bat.

Some part of his brain must have kicked in, because instead of going after his car, he threw the tool as far as he could down the street.

He stood still for a few minutes, his shoulders heaving and I got the impression of the Hulk trying to fight back against his anger. Then he stomped over to the door, slamming it so hard he broke off a piece of the frame.

Quincy shook his head and shut off the video. "That man's an animal. We have to keep him away from Zoey."

* * * *

I was early to my standing lunch with Tod, but he let me in anyway, his fascination with his latest puzzle—Benson's murder investigation—overriding his anxiety.

We sat down and started eating our Vietnamese sandwiches.

"Do you think this fixer really exists?" he asked after drinking half of his can of Coke in a few gulps. "I couldn't find anything about him online. Even on the dark web."

"Tod, please don't go on the dark web," I said. To me, it was like a horror film character running into the zombie infested forest.

"I know what I'm doing," he said. "Does Norma think Opal's death is connected to Benson's?"

"Well, they dated and possibly worked for the same person. Maybe they took money to do unethical things for students applying to college. But we don't have any idea why they were killed."

"It could be that they knew something the fixer doesn't want to get out," Tod said. "If he's real."

"Okay, that's a big 'if.' But let's just say he's out there. What does he hope to gain by getting rid of them? It's just bringing more attention to him," I said. "Now everyone's talking about a college 'fixer.'"

"Well, really, that's because of you," Tod said.

I went cold. He was right.

* * * *

The Osetra Seafood Restaurant glowed with an indigo blue light coming from the bar. It gave the whole restaurant a cool vibe and I felt like I was walking into a night club before it was packed with the kind of people who go to night clubs. Not that I knew anyone like that.

The host directed me to an upstairs area that had been set aside for the networking group, and I gave my name to a young woman standing at a podium handing out name tags.

A man about my age in a sports jacket over a button-down white shirt and crisp khakis came over to meet me. "Hi, I'm Clayton. You must be Colbie."

"How'd you know?" I asked, with my *nice to meet you* smile.

"You're the only newbie this month, so it was easy to figure out."

We both gave a fake laugh.

"It's so great that you started this group." I gestured around to all of the people holding drinks and chatting.

"Thank you," he said. "It just made sense to me since this industry changes so much."

"Oh yeah?" I asked. "How so?" As soon as it left my mouth, I realized it was the wrong thing to say. Anyone who took the time to attend this meeting should know that.

He tilted his head, and I rushed to cover for my flub. "I'm thinking of changing careers and someone recommended I start here."

He nodded. "Good idea."

Whew. I saved it.

He explained. "Every year it becomes harder to get into colleges, so every year our job becomes more challenging. You're staying for the speaker, right? Learning all you can about the SAT is one of the basics you'll need to make a go at this career." He sounded like an introduction to an infomercial.

"Thanks for including me," I said. "I definitely have a lot to learn."

He guided me to a small group and I explained again the fake reason I was there. A woman said, "Don't do it! Save yourself!" and they all laughed.

I was forced to respond to questions about why I was interested in moving into this field, but the group realized pretty quickly that I didn't have a clue about the industry and was of no use to them. They resumed their conversation about the difficulty of finding paid internships for high school students.

As soon as I could, I made my way to the bar and grabbed a glass of white wine so I could study the room. Clayton moved easily from group to group. He knew everybody. He just might be the key.

Soon, we gathered in one corner to listen to a speaker. Since a whiteboard wouldn't work in this setting, he'd printed out sample SAT tests and explained in far too much detail what the most recent changes were.

When it was finally over, I stayed behind to help Clayton, but besides handouts and name tags, there wasn't much to clean up. Time was up so I went for it. "Someone mentioned that there's a local college fixer helping students get into colleges they're not qualified for. Do you know anything about that?"

He turned toward me with a stunned look on his face. "What? Who said that?"

"I met so many people that I can't remember," I said. "I probably have to get better at remembering names." I laughed and started alphabetizing some name tags, pretending that my question wasn't all that important. "Anyway, he said that wealthy people will pay anything to anyone to get their kids into a great college, even a 'fixer.'" I made finger quote signs.

"That's impossible." He waved his hand as if pushing away the idea.

"Oh," I said. "That doesn't make sense. He said the guy was like *Ray Donovan*, you know, that TV show. I thought since you're so well-connected that you had to know him. Or about him at least."

"I've heard rumors, but that's it," he said.

More rumors. I felt a tingle on my neck.

"You should forget about him and focus on learning how to help the students," he said, trying to change the subject.

"Really? He exists?" I didn't have to pretend to be interested. "I knew you knew everyone. What have you heard?"

Just like I hoped, he responded to the approval. "That he operates some kind of unofficial network of people who can help smooth the way to college."

"How can he do that?" I asked.

"He gets high level business people and teachers to give glowing recommendations," he said. "I heard he can even get grades changed, but that's crazy."

"Hmm," I asked. "Does he work with music teachers?

He shrugged. "He might." Then he put the pieces together in his head. "No, wait. Are you a police officer?" He took a step one direction and then back. "Damn it. Ignore everything I said. I don't know anything."

"Clayton, calm down," I said. "I'm not a police officer. I'm helping out a friend and trying to learn what I can about this guy."

"Okay, okay," he said, getting himself under control. "Wait. You came here to talk about this?"

I didn't bothering answering that. "Just help me out for one minute," I said. "You know everyone, right? And I saw you work the room tonight. You are freaking incredible at connecting people. Connect the dots for me. What is this guy after? If he does exist, and it sounds like that part's true, then maybe he knew Benson Tadworth. I understand that it's a big if. The other big if is that if he knew Benson, what possible reason could he have to kill him? This is all hypothetical, because we don't even know if he's really out there."

"Oh man." He shook his head, but the appeal of the mystery pulled at him. "If it's true, then he must have a serious network connecting very different people for different reasons. He has to know someone at all of the schools. Plus technical people who can clean up social media and other sites. Local business leaders." He paused. "I don't know how he could manage something that big without people becoming aware of what he was doing."

"How do you think I could find this guy?" I asked, even though the thought made my heart pound.

He thought for a moment and then said, "I have a feeling he's the kind who finds you."

* * * *

Clayton had very little else to add, but the whole concept was beginning to take shape. Norma just had to figure out who else worked with this fixer, someone who was still alive, and use him or her to track the boss down.

Clayton's line *I have a feeling he's the kind who finds you* was beginning to creep me out, especially when I went into the almost empty Horton Plaza Garage. I came out on the wrong floor and had to walk up a ramp to find my car.

Beside it was a black BMW.

I stopped still, a strange warning prickle making the hair on my arms stand up. I instinctively backed up and hid behind a pillar halfway down the ramp, hoping the driver hadn't seen me.

Pulling out my phone, I bent over and awkwardly dashed back through the glass door, my lungs feeling so tight that I could only breathe in tiny gasps. I plastered myself against the wall and dialed Norma while peeking out.

Then the BMW drove by me, heading to the exit, and I pulled back so the driver couldn't see me. I hung up, thinking for a moment that I was worrying for no reason. The car windows were too dark to see inside, even when it passed under a fluorescent light.

Something about it was familiar. The glass was darkened well past the legal limit.

Then I remembered where I'd seen it. Outside Benson's house the morning I'd yelled at him.

I ran out and took a photo of the retreating car, hoping I caught the license plate. Then I redialed Norma's number.

"This is going to sound crazy," I said. "But I think someone did something to my car."

"Where are you?" she asked, and I could tell she was getting up from whatever she was doing to take action.

I told her where I was and about the BMW. A group of teens walked by, their chatting about a movie making me feel like I was probably overreacting.

"Stay on the line," she said. "I'm going to put you on hold for a minute."

I did as I was told, my fear giving way to embarrassment that I was worried about nothing.

Norma came back on. "I asked a patrol car to take a look, and I'm on my way."

Oh man. What if I imagined the whole thing? I walked back up the ramp and looked at my car. I felt the frisson of fear again. Maybe it was an overactive imagination.

"Did you see him do anything?" Norma asked.

I felt even more foolish, especially when I heard Norma starting her car. "No," I said. "Maybe I should go closer and look at it or something."

"No!" Norma said. "Trust your instincts. Stay away from the car."

Five minutes later, a patrol car pulled up and I waved the officers down.

They looked like they were still in their twenties, but were completely professional, both checking out the car from a distance and then moving closer. The shorter one dropped onto the ground to inspect underneath, and shook his head at the other that he didn't see anything. The other looked into the back seat and then stared at me. He called his partner over and pulled out his cell phone to take a photo of whatever was there.

My heart raced. "What is it?"

They both backed away from the car and then walked toward me. The shorter one called in an order, with numbers I didn't understand, but with an urgency that was clear.

The taller one held out his phone. "Do you recognize these people?"

I had to grab his phone and enlarge the photo, not really understanding what I was seeing. "What is that?"

"You have a bunch of photos in your back seat," he explained.

Suddenly, I could make sense of what I was seeing. Pictures. Of me, Elliott, my dad, Annie, Lani, Joss, and Kai.

I opened my mouth but all the air had left my lungs. My legs gave out and I would've fallen to the ground if the officer hadn't caught me.

"It's a threat," I said, when I could breathe again. "Against everyone I love."

Chapter 20

I was sitting inside the patrol car when Norma arrived, right after the bomb squad. She spoke to them briefly and came over to talk to me. One of the officers had found another GPS tracker on my car, hidden better this time. But at least they hadn't found a bomb.

She sat in the back with me but didn't say anything.

"Did you see the photo I sent you?" I asked.

She nodded. "We researched the license plate. Unfortunately, it's a counterfeit plate. The driver has probably switched it out by now."

The news didn't even faze me. Someone had tracked me to the meeting and decided that it was time to leave me an explicit warning.

Maybe they didn't like the kind of questions I was asking.

I'd been warned away from investigations before, and it was always when I was getting close to finding the murderer. But this time the murderer might as well be a ghost. It was most likely whoever was tracking and bugging me with military grade equipment. We had no way of knowing and no way to prove anything.

And even though I'd been warned before, nothing like this had ever happened. The photos shook me up. Someone had been following me and taking photos to use them for just this purpose.

Even though I was scared down to my bones, I couldn't help wondering how I could figure out who this sadistic jerk was. But I had an idea.

* * * *

The employees of A&D College Consulting did not get to work early. I figured that out when I arrived outside their offices before seven in the morning and sat looking at the green glass-enclosed small building for three hours in the parking lot. I'd borrowed my dad's car since mine was evidence once again.

Just as I was about to give up and go find a bathroom, a white Porsche drove up and out stepped Ian Luther. He looked just like the photo on the company website, down to the highlighted hair and tweed jacket with leather elbow patches.

"Mr. Luther?" I called out.

He turned and I was just about to congratulate myself on my stalking skills, when he took one look at my face and bolted for the front door.

What the heck?

I dashed after him, repeating his name. Luckily, the key gave him a little trouble and I was able to catch up. "What's wrong with you?" I demanded, and slid into the building with him before he could pull the door closed. I backed up against the door.

"I don't have time this morning," he said trying to sound haughty but coming across more frightened.

I pulled out copies of the photos that Norma had given me. "Too bad," I said. "I need to show you these. Someone left them in the back seat of my locked car."

His eyes closed briefly.

"You don't seem surprised by that," I said. "Do you know who these people are? That's my twelve year old son." I pointed to each person. "That's my boyfriend's ten year old daughter. That's my dad's seventy-five year old friend."

"Hold on." He walked over to turn off the security system that had started making warning beeps.

"Who is threatening me?" I asked. "You must know something."

"I can't tell you anything." He sounded distraught about it rather than mad.

"Is he some kind of college fixer?" I asked.

His face turned ashen and he sat down in a lobby chair with a low moan, his hands covering his face. "I'm not going to say another word. Except to tell you to go home and forget everything you know about him. I'm stuck with the devil, but you don't have to be. Save yourself."

* * * *

By the time I got home, Norma was probably already at A&D College Consulting. Ian might be able to stand up to me, but now that Norma knew this fixer was out there, she'd be ruthless. A few threats about warrants, and he'd be spilling everything he knew.

I hoped.

She'd also given me a photo from the security camera of a downtown Staples. A man with long hair wearing sunglasses and a baseball cap had printed out the photos using a machine in the corner. He'd kept his face angled away from the cameras but the photo she sent me was pretty good. I just had never seen him before.

The cashier had gotten a weird vibe from him, and thought the hair was a wig.

The fact that he used a store like that meant he hadn't been planning to ambush me with the photos. He saw me, or heard me, at the meeting and decided he needed to scare me off. For some reason, that made me feel a little better. Then I realized he may have been *at* the networking meeting and had simply slipped out early. The chill came back.

I checked in with Zoey and she said production was on schedule and I didn't need to come in. She hadn't heard anything from Red. In fact, her friend had gone to the same bar to get a read on him, and he'd never shown up.

I spent the afternoon catching up on accounting and making sure all of our ingredients were in stock.

I got ready early for my standing date night with Joss, deciding to wear a dress and heels. If Joss was going to say what I thought he was going to say, I wanted to treat it as a special occasion.

He came to my door wearing a nice blue button-down shirt, which matched his eyes, and black dress pants.

"You look beautiful," he said. He'd brought his car and we went to a wonderful Italian restaurant in La Mesa. He ordered Chianti and we shared the fried calamari appetizer.

"I heard the eggplant parmesan here is awesome," I said. "But did you see the size of those raviolis that went by?"

"Let's get both and split them," he suggested.

He grabbed my hand, brushing his thumb across it. "Have you heard anything about your proposal for those LA stores?"

By unspoken mutual agreement, we stayed away from any discussion on murder or exes. I had such a good time that I forgot he might be thinking of saying something important, until the drive home.

He cleared his throat. "Um, my house or home?"

"Well, I haven't seen the goats in days," I said.

He gave me a nervous smile, and I got concerned. Maybe he was ready to tell me something bad, not good. I pretended to be staring out at the scenery, which made no sense because it was dark. Finally, we got to his house and walked over to see the sleeping goats, who were still totally adorable, and then went inside.

He led the way into the living room, which he'd filled with candles. They were the fake kind, so he didn't risk burning the house down. The whole room glowed with warm flickering lights. A bottle of champagne was set in an ice holder on the coffee table, beside a large vase of red roses.

"Wow. This is amazing," I said. "Did I forget our anniversary or something?"

He paused as if doing math in his head. "It might be, but that's not what this is about."

He pulled me close and leaned his forehead against mine. "I want you to know something I've been feeling for a while, but haven't had the courage to tell you."

I stayed silent, my heart in my throat, and looked into his eyes.

"I love you," he said.

Even though I'd hoped for it, I was still stunned. I'm pretty sure my face got all melty just like a cartoon character's does, and that little hearts started floating around my head. "I love you too."

I kissed him and my phone rang. This time I ignored it.

"Hold on," he said. He grabbed both of our phones and put them on the porch.

Then he came back in and kissed me until I was breathless.

* * * *

I snuck into my house after midnight, and even though I was exhausted, I couldn't stop smiling.

Then Zoey called and I knew something was terribly wrong. "Colbie," she whispered. "He's here."

A chill ran down my spine. "Call the police," I said. "And tell me where you are." I dug for my dad's keys.

"I called them," she said. "I don't know why I called you."

"Tell me the address," I insisted. "I'll be right there."

"4545 Cabot Street," she said. "He's singing at the top of his lungs outside. You can't miss him."

I ran outside, not stopping to lock the door. "I'm on my way. Stay on the phone with me."

"Shit," she said, sounding panicked. "I think he saw me."

"Stay away from the windows," I said, but it was too late.

"What the—" Whatever she was about to say was drowned out by the sound of breaking glass.

"Oh my God." Her voice was a frightened sob. "He's coming in!"

"Run!" I yelled. "Get out of there!" I started the car and peeled out without putting my seat belt on.

I could hear Red clearly in the background. "You cheating bitch! You always thought you were the good one, but now we know the truth, don't we." His words were slurred.

Then I heard a slap followed by a scream and a thump that made me go cold. The phone went dead and I drove faster, screeching around the corners, my heart pounding as I chanted "too slow, too slow," over and over. Then I saw the Cabot Street sign and with one last turn, I slammed to a stop. Six police cars had their headlights pointed at the house.

Red was holding Zoey in front of him, his arm around her neck. She was on her tip-toes, struggling to find purchase on the ground so she could breathe. Blood ran from her mouth.

They were surrounded, a dozen guns pointed at them, but Red wasn't giving up.

Then Zoey sagged down and her body went limp.

"No!" I yelled.

He nearly dropped her, her dead weight too much for him, but at least his grip loosened.

I yelled, "Shoot him!" but then Zoey came alive. She bit his arm, hard, and he screamed, then she slipped away from him, and took an attack stance I'd only seen in movies. She bounced on her feet twice, and went into a flying round house kick that connected with his face.

His head jerked back, taking his body with him to the ground. She completed her circle in the air and landed on both feet, keeping her eyes focused on him.

A couple of the police started to move in, but someone in charge yelled, "Stay back!"

Red struggled to get to his feet, his knees buckling before he could stand. He screamed and lunged at her.

Zoey danced back a step, and he missed her completely. Then she got to work, hitting and kicking him with martial arts combinations that sent him to his knees.

She bounced on her toes, watching him carefully, the headlights of the police cars making her the star attraction. Then she grabbed him by his hair, pulled his head up to look him in the eyes, said something I couldn't hear, and then slammed his face into the ground.

The police swarmed both of them, and I ran as close to her as I could get. She was heaving, pulling in air in big breaths. Steam rose off of her body as she wiped the blood from her mouth.

She looked like an Amazon, like every woman who wanted to avenge her hurts.

A woman officer told her to put her hands on the car and Zoey followed her orders.

"You did it," I said. "You kicked his ass." I yelled to her as another officer forced me to move back. The words seemed so small compared to the victory.

She turned her head to meet my eyes and nodded, her expression intense.

The officer put handcuffs on Zoey and led her to one of the police cars. I heard her say something about making a statement.

"Don't answer any questions. Don't say a word," I shouted, "until your lawyer gets there!"

I looked down at the battered pulp of Red, his groaning giving me mixed feelings. He was a waste of human skin, but I didn't want Zoey to go to jail. He turned on his side in a fetal position, his arms wrapped around what had to be multiple broken ribs. There was no way he was bothering her ever again.

Zoey had already made her statement.

Chapter 21

I called Quincy right away and followed the car Zoey was in to the police station. Quincy's lawyer arrived less than an hour later.

Stuck in the waiting room, I texted Lani with what had happened. Of course, she was asleep and didn't answer.

Two women officers seemed to be talking about Zoey as they walked by. "I say that girl's a freakin' hero."

The other one said, "We should get her to work here."

You can't have her, I wanted to tell them.

Then I got a phone call from Zoey's phone and I quickly picked it up. "This is the San Diego Police. We understand you received a call from this number earlier tonight?"

I hung up. I wasn't saying a word until I talked to Quincy's lawyer. Fortunately, he walked out to the lobby to bring me in the back to make a statement. "Just tell them exactly what you heard over the phone."

It was much harder than I thought it would be. My emotions kept seesawing between absolute terror and rage at the man who had hurt her.

The lawyer patted me on the back when I was done, so I assumed I helped Zoey's case.

At three in the morning, Zoey was released on her "own recognizance." She walked into the lobby, holding ice to her cheek, with a butterfly bandage on her forehead. When she saw me she smiled.

Then she swore, as the cut in her lip opened up and started bleeding again.

I rushed over to hug her, being as gentle as I could. "I was so scared," I said.

"Me too," she said. "And then I wasn't."

Her lawyer signed some papers and came over to us. "I assume you're taking Zoey home?" He didn't wait for an answer. "I should learn your court date next week. You stay out of trouble until you appear before the judge and you should be fine. As long as he lives, that is."

My eyes widened. "He was alive when we left."

"That's good," he said. "Let's hope he stays that way."

I drove Zoey to where Zeke was staying. Her friend was delighted to have her come in, even at that hour, and I headed home. She sent me a picture of Zeke sleeping peacefully, and I finally felt like they would be okay.

* * * *

I put aside work and everything about Benson's murder to begin preparation for the Thanksgiving feast. Any time my brain drifted that way, I brought it back by thinking about Joss and last night. Which led me to Zoey. I'd be nervous about her until she was cleared of any wrongdoing. I hadn't even called Norma back, even though she might have news.

Trouble was going crazy wondering why I wasn't giving her tastes, but I was only handling the prep work today. The dining room was back to normal, except for the occasional pushpins I kept finding with my bare feet, and the glitter that I knew would be there as long as the house existed.

Elliott came downstairs while I was setting the table, one of the many chores I could do early so I wouldn't have to worry about it while I was cooking on the big day.

"Hey, Mom?" he asked, in a tone that I knew meant he wanted to ask me something. Something that I wouldn't like.

"Hey, bud," I said. "What's up?"

"Dad just called," he said.

I held back the *uh-oh* that I wanted to say. "Okay."

"He was supposed to go to San Francisco today to join the rest of his family, but there's something wrong with his plane. It's, like, grounded."

"O-kay." That word came out very slowly.

"Can he join us for Thanksgiving?" He looked up at me with puppy eyes and I was lost.

Are you kidding me? I wanted to scream. Instead, I glanced at my dad who was staring at me wide-eyed. He gave me an *it's up to you* shrug. Wonderful.

"Sure," I said.

"Great! Thank you!" He gave me a quick hug and then ran back up to his room to tell his dad.

"This is going to be an interesting Thanksgiving," my dad said, shaking his head.

My phone rang. It was Kai. That was weird. She'd never called me before, but Joss had asked me to keep her number in my phone in case of an emergency.

I picked it up. "Kai?"

"I'm sorry. It's Gemma."

Oh man. What did she want now? "Hi," I said, keeping my tone even. My dad was staring at me and I mouthed her name.

He laughed, covering his mouth with his hand so she wouldn't hear.

"I know this is terrible, trying to take advantage like this, and I know that Joss would never bother you with this. But Kai recently asked if we would ever be able to celebrate a holiday together. And I just wondered, you can say no, really. But I wanted to find out if there's any way I could come to Thanksgiving tomorrow."

My jaw actually dropped. I covered the phone and whispered, "She wants to come tomorrow!" to my dad.

He laughed even louder and then said, "Why not?" Not a good *"Why not?"* but a *"This is already crazy. Why not add more crazy to it? Why not?"*

I failed to see the humor.

"Of course, if it's too hard for you, I totally understand," she said in a sickly sweet tone.

What a witch. But she'd backed me into a corner. "Sure," I said. "Three o'clock."

We hung up and I immediately called Lani. "We're all grown-ups." I tried to make myself feel less horror-stricken. "It'll be fine."

"Don't worry," she said. "Piper and I will be on 'ew' duty and we'll totally handle her."

"Oo duty?" I asked.

"E. W., for ex-wife," she said. "But we say 'ew' because she stinks as a human being."

I laughed. "Just don't say it by accident tomorrow."

Next I dialed Joss. "So I have some bad news and some bad news. What do you want first?"

"The bad news?" he asked.

"Richard is joining us for Thanksgiving." I explained about his plane.

"Okay," he said, drawing out the word as if he was considering all of the ramifications. "What's the other bad news?"

"So is Gemma."

"What?" His voice got much sharper with that revelation.

I told him about her phone call, blaming Kai more than Gemma in an effort to keep the peace.

He was quiet for a minute.

"You okay?" I asked.

"This is going to be the most stressful Thanksgiving in the history of the holiday," he said.

"From what I understand, that bar is pretty high."

* * * *

My dad was delighted that Joss and I had said the "L word." But on Thanksgiving morning, he realized that it might cause things between us to change.

"You know you don't have to worry about me, right?" he said. "I don't want you to feel obligated to live here and not, you know, live your own life." He was sitting in his chair with his feet up, drinking his first of many beers of the day.

"Dad, we're not even close to anything like that," I said. "And just so you know, I can't imagine moving out. Elliott and I love it here."

"Okay," he said. "Don't just stay because you think it'll hurt my feelings or something."

I hugged him from behind. "I love you, Dad."

He patted my arm. "I love you too." Then he cleared his throat and said, "I can't see the parade."

* * * *

"Are we going to be able to handle this?" I asked Joss when he came into the kitchen for refills. I was deep in food prep, moving along according to the detailed schedule I'd prepared, and the whole house smelled amazing, like turkey and stuffing and pie all at the same time.

Richard was sitting in the living room with Elliott, my dad, and Annie. They were all watching a football game and actually talking. Both Richard and Joss had surfed a lot when they were younger, so they'd found something they had in common to talk about besides Elliott and me.

Elliott was hanging out with Kai who was trying to get Trouble to stay on the couch with her. The cat kept jumping down to look at the bookcase in the corner of the living room.

"You can handle anything," Joss said, keeping his voice low. "But the only thing that'll keep me sane is thinking about Saturday." He kissed my cheek and grabbed two beers and two sodas from the refrigerator, which was a lot emptier now that the turkey was in the oven.

Since Elliott was going to San Francisco with Richard and Kai was spending the rest of the weekend with Gemma's family, Joss had surprised me by inviting me to Temecula for the weekend. The plan was to go wine tasting and stay at a beautiful bed-and-breakfast.

"Stop giving each other googly eyes and tell me if this cranberry sauce is thick enough," Lani said from the stove.

"It looks awesome," I said as Joss went back to the living room. I grabbed a spoon and, after blowing on it a few times, tasted it. "It's perfect. Sweet and tangy and delicious."

Today Lani was wearing a brown sweater over a beige skirt with small designs on it. Pretty low-key for her. Then I looked closer. "Are those turkeys?" I asked.

"Yep. Appropriate, right?" She glanced up at the clock above the sink. "Piper should be here soon." Then she looked at me. "Don't be insulted by what I'm about to tell you. Because this ensures that your life is less complicated, and you could sure use less complications these days right?"

"Oh my God, yes."

"Bio-dad, I mean, Richard, is not at all interested in you," she said, as if delivering excellent news.

"I know," I said. Something about it felt weird though, not that I was admitting it to anyone.

"It doesn't make a lot of sense, because look at you." She gestured both hands toward me. "You're gorgeous and smart and accomplished. And kind. But it's really good because Joss is awesome and you don't want anything to mess with that."

"He really is, isn't he?" I said it like a question that I knew the answer to.

I checked my phone for the fifth time in an hour and saw a text from Zoey. "Oh good."

"What?" Lani asked.

"I invited Zoey and Zeke for dinner, but they're spending the day with friends," I said. "She said her face was feeling a lot better."

I'd told Lani everything, and then repeated the story for my dad and again for Joss. Lani couldn't believe that Quincy had come up with the whole elaborate plan to convince Red that he wasn't Zeke's father, but she agreed that it was necessary. Quincy felt terribly guilty that he hadn't predicted Red's violent response, but Zoey told him that she'd agreed to the plan too so if it was Quincy's fault, it was her fault. And nothing Red did was her fault.

I was glad that I'd told Gemma to arrive right when dinner was being served. She stood in the kitchen doorway wearing a short black skirt and a silky red shirt that showed a lot of cleavage.

Whoa.

"Ignore it," Lani whispered as she walked by me to welcome Gemma. "Colbie's finishing up the mashed potatoes and then we'll sit down."

"Do you need any help?" Gemma asked, but didn't seem to mean it.

"I'm good," I said overly cheerful. "Lani, can you get Gemma some wine or beer?"

"Sure thing." Lani poured her a glass of chardonnay and eased her toward the living room.

I breathed a sigh of relief, even knowing it was temporary, and started up the hand mixer again.

Lani came back and said, "You trust me, right? I just saw Joss's face when Gemma sat down. Right beside him, of course. And I am one hundred percent sure that he's not interested in her." She held up two fingers. "Scouts honor. You have nothing to worry about."

I smiled, feeling some amount of relief even though I knew it was true.

We brought the food to the table, which practically groaned under the weight, and invited everyone to sit down.

Elliott opened up my laptop and set it on one of the kitchen bar stools at the edge of the table. Soon Tod's face appeared on the screen. "Happy Thanksgiving everyone," Tod said. His voice was quiet as if he was embarrassed.

Everyone responded in a chorus of "Happy Thanksgiving to you" and he smiled.

"So glad you can make it, Tod," I said. Maybe next year he'd actually be here.

Lani directed people to their chairs. My dad was at the head of the table with Annie beside him. Elliott and Kai sat together. I was at the foot of the table with Joss. Gemma made a move to sit beside him, and Lani pointed to the open seat beside Richard. "That's your seat, Gemma."

I widened my eyes. She wasn't pushing her on Richard, was she?

She read my mind, or my expression, and said quietly as she sat down beside me, "He's not interested in her either."

Annie started Thanksgiving by saying, "I have a tradition that I'd like to suggest. We should all go around the table and say one thing that we're grateful for. I'll start. I'm grateful that I found love again and that I have such wonderful neighbors who make me feel like family."

Richard cleared his throat. "I was going to say something about not having to face vegan Thanksgiving in San Francisco, but you had to get serious on me."

Everyone laughed.

He looked at Elliott. "I'm so very grateful to have my son in my life, for getting to know what a wonderful young man he is." He paused, as if his feelings were getting the best of him, and continued with difficulty. "And especially that he and Colbie were big enough people to forgive me."

Elliott said, "Me too." He blew out a breath and then said, "And for getting to live here with my grandpa."

Kai said, "I'm grateful for my goats!"

Everyone laughed again, a relief from the complicated emotions swirling around the room.

Gemma said, "You're welcome, sweetie," completely missing the point, but I held back my eye roll.

She started to say something and then stopped herself. "I'm grateful to be starting a new career," she finished simply.

"Hey Tod," I said. "Want to go next?"

He took a deep breath. "I'm grateful for the progress I made this year," he said. Then he held up a turkey leg, "And for online food delivery services!"

The chuckles around the table were heartwarming.

"We want to go last," Lani said, and Piper smiled, turning to my dad.

"I'm grateful for a lot of things," he said. "Having my daughter and grandson living here with me is a great joy, along with sharing my life with Annie." He shook his head as if he couldn't believe his luck, and tears gathered in his eyes.

Seeing anyone cry, especially my dad, always made me cry. I wiped away a few tears, and Joss grabbed my hand.

"This has been a wonderful year for all of us, hasn't it?" Joss said. "Every minute I share with Kai is a treasure. You have all become so much more than neighbors, you've become friends, and even family. I'm grateful to have you all in my life, especially Colbie, who has brought love and adventure into every day."

I took a deep breath. "You guys have used up all the good stuff, so I'm just going to say 'ditto.' This is a wonderful time for family and friends and I just want it to continue."

"I can't wait anymore!" Lani said as Piper shook her head with affection. "Guess what we're grateful for? We're having a baby!"

The table erupted into cheers and well-wishes. I jumped to my feet and ran around the table to hug them both.

Chapter 22

When I woke up the next morning, I felt wonderful. The turkey had come out great, flavorful and moist. Everyone had eaten until they were stuffed. We took a break from gorging to rest. Joss and Piper had loaded the dishwasher, "because they hadn't helped to cook."

That worked for me. At halftime during the second football game, we felt like we might have enough room for more food. We went back to the dining room for pumpkin pie piled high with whipped cream.

Gemma had stayed quiet most of the time, and she and Kai left as soon as possible while still being polite. I think she realized that regardless of what happened between Joss and me, she was never getting him back. I didn't expect to see her around his farm much more.

It wasn't until I saw Trouble staring at the bookcase in the living room again that the memory of the fixer came back to me, along with the feeling that we were being watched.

Tod had told me it wasn't possible for Trouble to sense electronic surveillance but I wasn't taking any chances. I waited for it to be a decent hour and texted him. *Could your friend have missed one?*

He knew what I meant. *The RF detectors aren't perfect, but I think it's unlikely*, he texted back. *Why?*

I didn't want to argue with him about Trouble's talent in sensing the bugs. *Can you send him over again?*

Sure.

A short time later, he texted, *One hour.*

Make it two, I responded.

And then I plotted.

* * * *

A short time later, Richard arrived to pick up Elliott for their trip to San Francisco. His plane was still grounded but he'd arranged to rent another private plane. I didn't even know that was possible. His family, which I guess meant Elliott's new family, was holding a second Thanksgiving dinner for both of them.

Richard had gone into the living room to shake my dad's hand and thank him for his hospitality for Thanksgiving.

"Colbie did all the work," my dad said.

"We should go," Richard said to Elliott. "We want to get out before the rain hits."

I smiled and hugged Elliott a little tighter.

"You okay?" he asked.

"I'm good," I said. "Still stuffed from yesterday, but good."

"I'm not!" he said.

"Thanks for letting him go with me," Richard said, holding the front door open for Elliott.

"You're welcome," I said. I smiled and waved good-bye from the porch until they turned the corner. The empty street made me feel bereft.

I went back inside to wait for the Wizard.

Even though I suspected that there was another bug in my living room, it still pissed me off when he found it taped to the top of one of the shelves in the bookcase. I shook my head at him to leave it there and asked him to check the whole house again.

The Wizard also analyzed my phone. "Still clean."

I went outside to call Norma and asked her to meet me for coffee.

She said, "No time." She hung up.

I called her back. "You have time for this," I insisted and told her about the new bug.

When I arrived at Philz, she was shaking out her umbrella. The sky was dark gray with rain clouds working overtime to fix the drought in southern California.

This time she bought the coffee and we sat at the long counter in front that looked out over the parking lot. I left my phone in my car even though the Wizard said it was safe.

"Okay, hear me out," I said. "We know that someone with access to military grade surveillance equipment is following me. What about if we used that to flush him out?"

She narrowed her eyes and sipped her coffee. "Explain."

"Whoever this guy is, he knows that we know there's some kind of fixer around here," I said. "But no one knows who he is. If it gets too hard for him to do business, he can just leave town and start this whole thing up somewhere else."

"Not if I can help it." Her voice was grim.

"He's been ahead of us the whole time," I reminded her. "There are lots of rich people all over the country who would use his services."

She crossed her arms.

I took a deep breath and told her my plan.

"It's too dangerous," she argued.

"Norma, this nameless, faceless fixer is giving me the creeps every single day. We have to catch him."

"You don't even know if that's who's bugging you," she said.

"And tracking me," I reminded her.

"Or even responsible for Benson's death."

"That's exactly why we need my plan," I said. "Even if he decides to roll up his little network and get out of town, he might be the kind of person who doesn't like to leave loose ends behind. We have to flush him out or I'll be looking over my shoulder for a long time. I don't want to live like that."

She looked down at the counter, considering it. Then she looked out the window at the rain and considered it some more.

Then she said, "Okay."

* * * *

First, I told my dad to take Annie to a double feature at the movies. He looked at me funny but did it.

Then the Wizard got to work, putting a wire on both Norma and me, and installing a bunch of bugs in Benson's house, along with tiny cameras. We were going to draw the fixer out and capture him in Benson's house. It was weirdly poetic, like a neat justice circle.

Yollie stopped by and I brought her into my living room, right by the bookcase. "Here's that recording," she said, doing a great job of following the script and sounding natural. "I couldn't make much of it out but maybe your detective friend can."

"What could you hear?" I asked.

"It sounded like a threat," she said. "But it was kinda muffled. I bet the police can do that magic stuff like they do on TV and make it really clear."

"Thanks," I said. "I'll call Norma."

We said our good-byes and I called Norma, putting her on speaker phone. "Hi Norma, I think you're going to want to send someone over for this. Um, I'll call you right back. Someone else is calling."

Right on schedule, Fabiola, Benson's housekeeper, called. I put her on speakerphone too. "I remembered something," she said. "Benson had a hiding place. He was really mad that I disturbed it by accident one day." Her Italian accent was more pronounced, maybe because she was nervous.

"What's in it?" I asked.

"A bunch of tapes," she said. "He said it was insurance, but that doesn't make sense. He didn't sell insurance."

"That is weird," I said. "Where's the hiding place?"

"It's in the back of the antique cabinet in the corner of the dining room," she said. "It has a trick door but you can see a hook if you look closely."

"Thanks for letting me know." I spoke clearly.

We hung up and I dialed Norma to relay the new information. My hope was that whoever was listening on the other side of that bug would be worried about what was on Steven's recording and even more worried about Benson's tapes.

"Damn it, I need to get another warrant. Can you meet me at Benson's in an hour?" Norma asked. "And bring the recording."

"Sure," I said.

I paced the house, looking out all of the windows to see if I could see anyone. Nothing seemed out of the ordinary. Trouble shadowed me, occasionally meowing. *What the heck are you doing? It's not going to go the way you think it will.*

I might have been projecting my worries onto her.

Exactly forty minutes later, I ran out to my dad's car, getting totally soaked on the way. I started the engine, and flicked the windshield wipers on. They had a hard time keeping up with the rain.

"You okay?" I asked as I pulled out of the driveway.

"Quiet," Norma said from her hiding place on the back seat. She was covered with a blanket the same color as the interior.

I slowly drove toward Benson's house, wondering what the cameras were catching there. I stopped at a stop sign. Right past the intersection, a fast-moving sheet of water ran down a hill on one side, across the street and down into the steep canyon on the other side. I drove into the water slowly, worried about how deep it really was. Then I heard the loud sound of a gunning engine.

I looked up in time to see a large pickup truck with an oversized grill crash into my side of the car. It kept going, pushing us right over the side of the road into the canyon.

Chapter 23

The car continued sliding down the muddy hillside, coming to a stop against the trunk of a small tree halfway down the slope. "Are you okay?" I yelled to Norma.

"I'm fine," she said. "You?"

"I think so," I said. "My leg hurts."

She swore. "We're lucky the car didn't roll."

Oh man. I didn't even think of that. Sliding so far in the mud was bad enough.

She peered up the hill through the rain. "Someone is coming. He has to be coming for the recording. I'm going to circle around and get him from behind. Got it?"

I was so scared that I couldn't answer.

"Colbie," she said, her voice calm and sure. "Trust me. It'll be okay. Just keep him talking."

"Wait!" I said. I hit the button that would keep the interior lights from going on. "Okay, now."

She was out the door on the other side in a flash, sliding to the ground, and gently closing the door again. I had to hold myself back from begging her to stay with me. This was definitely not going according to plan.

The sound of the rain on the car changed from a dull roar to a hiss as it eased up, and I could hear my heart pounding. Then it stopped for one full beat when I saw someone sliding down the slope in the mud.

I whimpered and had to remind myself to play my part.

Even after he was standing right beside the car in his jacket with the hood up, it took me a long time to recognize him. Drake, the pyramid scam guy from Chubby's Pizza and the farmers' market.

"Drake? What are you doing here? Call 911!" I realized he couldn't hear me and reached out slowly to open the window a couple of inches. Rain water splashed in, the angle of my car allowing it to pour down the inside of the door. "Drake? Can you help me get out? My leg is stuck."

"Give me the recording," he said, his tone vicious. He pulled a gun out of the back of his jeans and pointed it at me. It was so close, I could see the rain drops falling on it and bouncing off.

"What?" I shook my head like I was confused. "Wait. You're the one following me? You put the tracker on my car? Why?"

"I'm careful and I do my research," he said. "I thought you might be trouble. So I kept an eye on you." He had a buzz cut under the hood and he no longer had a beer belly. His big hands held the gun like he knew what to do with it. The whole goofy guy persona had been a disguise, and I'd fallen for it.

I remembered the last time we met at Chubby's. I'd introduced him to Elliott. He shook my son's hand. I shuddered. "But the tow truck guy found it and took it off," I whined.

He scowled at me. "I hid the next one better."

Of course. "I'm so confused. I think I hit my head." I made my voice weak. "So you're the one who killed Benson?"

He stepped closer. "Don't act stupid. It won't work."

I had to keep him talking. "What did Benson ever do to you?"

"Benson killed himself," he said. "Now hand it over."

"That doesn't make any sense." I sat up straight and reached for my purse.

"Easy there," he said.

"I don't have a gun. Oh, you probably know that," I said. I didn't have to act to sound terrified. I was frightened to my bones. "My theory is that he got mad that the student went back on his deal and he was going to rescind the recommendation to help get his reputation back. Maybe even expose you." I reluctantly dug in my purse, pulling out a small bottle of water and some used tissues.

"You've been very productive," he said. "Especially for a soccer mom. I underestimated you."

He still hadn't admitted anything for the microphone.

I pulled out a notebook and a half-empty pack of sugarless chewing gum. "What do you mean Benson killed himself?" I peered into the purse, as if actually trying to find something.

"He said he had proof of our relationship. He freaked out when I was holding that tool and rammed his own damn neck into it." He shook his head in disgust.

I didn't react, but inside my stomach clenched at his matter-of-fact tone. "But what about Opal?" I pulled out three pens and a protein bar wrapper. "What happened to her?"

"She made the mistake of trying to blackmail me," he said.

Then I remembered why I was even at Chubby's. "You put crickets in Pico's restaurant!" I said. "Why'd you have to go and do that?"

"You were too protected there," he said. "Now give me the recording."

There was only one reason he was telling me all this. He didn't expect me to be around to tell anyone. Where was Norma? I moved slower, pulling out one program from *The Lion King*, and then another. This was going to take a while. I'd seen the play five times.

"That's enough delaying," he said. "Just give me the damn purse." He reached in to grab it and Norma stepped up behind him, holding her gun to the back of his head. "Drop the gun."

His face turned red with anger and he didn't move for a moment, as if he was contemplating shooting me anyway.

I didn't move, scared senseless.

Norma pushed harder, grinding the barrel against his skull. "Now."

Sirens rang out from the top of the hill, along with the sound of doors slamming and people yelling.

He threw the gun into the mud, and police officers swarmed down the hill. I sagged with relief, starting to cry in earnest.

* * * *

Lani stopped by the next morning, bringing my favorite peach and mango donuts to my perch on the couch.

"Hey Momma," I said.

She gave me a brilliant smile. "How are you feeling?"

I pointed to my leg which I had propped up on some pillows. "Other than a bruised leg, I'm good."

My bag was packed and Joss would be picking me up soon for our trip to Temecula. I'd been cleared by the doctor for fine dining and wine tasting, but not hiking. Two days all by ourselves in a beautiful area with nothing to worry about? It seemed like heaven.

Lani sat down on the other end of the couch, and Trouble left me to be petted by someone new. "Tell me everything." She picked up the cat and put her in her lap.

"Well, our plan kind of worked," I said. I'd been worried that Norma would get in trouble for not only agreeing to it, but also for being such a big part of it.

Norma had told me she'd be fine. "We got him and no one else died," she'd said.

"Your harebrained plan," Lani interjected. "We really should have held that intervention."

"We just didn't expect him to go after us on the way there," I complained. "I guess we should have thought it through a little better."

"No kidding," she said. "Tell me about this Drake guy."

"Drake Frost is actually Duncan Foster, an ex-Army intelligence guy who decided to use his skills to cash in on the whole college craze." My voice was light, but talking about him still made me shudder inside.

"I can't believe there really was a fixer." She shook her head in amazement.

"It took me too long to believe it," I said. "It still sounds like a movie instead of real life."

Someone on Twitter already said they were writing a screenplay.

"Did he really make a million dollars a kid, like that A&D employee said?" she asked. "And are you ever going to tell me who he or she was?"

"No," I said. "And I don't think Norma's figured that out yet. But he was throwing around a lot of cash, so he must have made a ton."

"Enough to justify murder in his own twisted head, I guess," she said.

I paused for a minute, remembering the scene in the car. "He told me that Benson's death was an accident." I almost believed him. But then he'd killed Opal and would've killed me if it wasn't for Norma.

She blew out a scoffing breath. "Right."

"He said he was holding the mandrel against Benson's neck. That Benson fought to get away and it went into his neck." My voice shook. Saying it brought back the memory of finding Benson's body and the garage blowing up.

"Ouch." She winced. "Do you think a jury will buy it?"

"Probably not," I said. "Especially since he blew up the place to get rid of any evidence."

"And he didn't care who else got hurt," she said, indignant. "That was before we had any rain. It was so dry, the whole neighborhood could have burned down. Or worse."

"Well, now he's being charged with two murders and arson," I said.

"I hope he never gets out," Lani said.

"You want to hear the most interesting part?" I asked. "Norma said that what he was doing—all the grade-changing and buying recommendation letters—wasn't actually illegal."

"What? It has to be," she said.

"I know, right?" I said. "If he hadn't killed Benson and Opal, he wouldn't be going to jail."

"Someone's got to fix that," she said. "For lack of a better word. It's like a big old loophole for unethical college counselors to drive through."

"I'm pretty sure that Sunnyside High School, and maybe a lot of other schools, are going to do a grade audit for the last few years, since no one knows when any of this started. If they find any discrepancies, those students might lose their place in college and even their scholarships."

"That's a fitting punishment," she said. "Hey, have you heard from Zoey?"

I nodded. "Yeah, she said her lawyer thinks she'll be let off since it was clearly self-defense. All of the police who were there seem to be on her side."

"And Zeke?"

"She said he's great."

"She better tell him never to send his DNA into one of the Ancestry places," she said.

I laughed. "That's true. But knowing the kind of guy Red is, he probably doesn't want his DNA information stored by one of those services either."

"Okay, last question," she said. "Any news on your big business proposal?"

"Nothing concrete," I said. "But Quincy's contact said they're leaning toward accepting it. I won't believe it until it actually happens. If it happens."

"Well, if karma has anything to do with it, they'll say yes." She stood up and Trouble protested. *Bring back my lap.*

She bent over to hug me. "If anyone deserves good things to happen to them, it's you."

"Thanks."

She let go and stood up. "I have to go. Piper has an ultrasound today. We get to see our little baby bean again." Her face beamed with happiness. "Can you please keep yourself safe for a little while?"

"I'm definitely taking a break from mysteries, for the weekend at least," I assured her with a laugh.

With perfect timing, Joss called.

I held up the phone to show Lani. "I'm choosing romance."

If you enjoyed

The Trouble with Talent,

look for the first

Gourmet Cat Mystery

For a peek at *The Trouble with Murder,*

turn the page and enjoy!

Available at your favorite e-retailers.

Chapter 1

A chicken rang the doorbell.

I stood in the open doorway, a little dumbfounded, and stared down at the beige bird with a mop of floppy feathers on its head that looked like a hat. The kind of hat women wore as a half joke to opening day at the horse races. How could it even see through that thing? And did it really just ring the doorbell?

Braving the mid-morning heat of Sunnyside, California, inland from downtown San Diego by twenty miles and what felt like twenty degrees hotter, I stuck my head out and looked up and down my dad's street. No teens were hanging around, giggling over their prank.

The chicken ruffled its whole body as if to say, "Yes, it was me." The *you idiot* was implied by the way it poked his beak toward me and then scratched its feet on the wooden porch floor.

"Right." I spoke out loud. To a chicken. I had to get out of the house more.

I'd been up since four in the morning, grinding various chicken parts and cooking them for my organic cat food business, and I was already tired. Maybe this was a poultry hallucination brought on by exhaustion. Or induced by guilt.

Maybe this was the king of the chicken underworld, seeking retribution for what was going on in my kitchen.

I shook my head. I had to stop reading so many of those horror novels my bloodthirsty twelve-year-old son, Elliott, couldn't get enough of.

My dad shuffled over to stand beside me, tugging his bathrobe tighter around his waist. "Hey, Charlie," he said.

I raised my eyebrows. He was talking to a bird too. "A boy bird?" I asked. Was that really the most important thing about the chicken on our doorstep?

The chicken ignored both of us, now finding the railing fascinating enough to peck.

"Of course he's a boy bird," he said, his Boston accent coming through. "He's one of Joss's Buff Laces."

"What?"

"His chickens. This is a Buff Laced Polish chicken," he said. "Look at that comb."

"Comb?" I asked.

"That foofy thing on the top of his head," he told me.

The comb in question was quite remarkable, but what did I know about chickens?

"How did it, he, make it to the doorbell?" I thought chickens didn't fly. Wasn't that the whole point of them? Food that can't fly away?

"Charlie was owned by some shrink at a college or something," he said, his normal morning mad-scientist hair almost matching the bird's.

As if to demonstrate, Charlie flapped his wings, getting enough lift to hop onto the planter with some drooping lavender in it. He stretched out his neck to poke his beak at the doorbell. It took a few tries but then he got it, tilting his head as though he was listening to the "Yankee Doodle" tune that made me grind my teeth every time I heard it, and then hopped down, looking up at me expectantly.

Maybe this one was some kind of X-Games chicken.

"Does he want a treat?" I asked my dad.

Then my cat, Trouble, gave a low warning snarl that Charlie seemed to recognize because he turned around and fluttered down the steps in half-flight-half-run. I grabbed Trouble just as she was about to chase after the poor bird, and handed her to my dad. "Take her," I said. "I'll make sure Charlie gets home."

Trouble had been an apartment cat and hadn't been very curious about the outside world until we moved out of the city to my dad's house. Now we had to make sure she didn't escape every time we opened a door.

My dad held Trouble with his hands outstretched, looking unsure. Which was probably because she was still in full battle mode and swatted at me as soon as she could twist around in his arms, screeching, *"Let me at 'em."*

Not really, but I knew what she meant.

"She'll calm down in a minute," I told my dad as I dashed after the chicken.

Charlie was sticking to the sidewalk, but headed in the opposite direction from his home. After the doorbell stunt, I imagined he knew his way around town. But it wasn't up to me to keep him safe on an adventure. I just wanted to get him back to his pen.

Within seconds, I was dripping with sweat and regretting not grabbing my sunglasses. The glare of the mid-morning sun irritated my eyes that already felt scratchy from lack of sleep.

I ran in front of Charlie and attempted to sheep-dog him back the other way. He scooted around me.

"Damnit," I said, and hustled to get past him. He must have decided it was a race because he started running, determined to reach his goal, whatever that was.

I got in front of him, my huffing and puffing making me realize I should get back to the gym, and yelled, "Shoo!" while waving my arms like a...like a chicken.

He came to a stop in the most theatrical, wings flapping, squawking protest the world had ever seen, and reversed course.

"Drama queen," I said, hoping he didn't keep up the complaining all the way back. I hadn't yet met our neighbor, Joss Hayden, but something made me think that a certified organic farmer might not like me upsetting his chicken. Of course, I'd heard all about him from my dad, who said he was the best neighbor ever, occasional chicken coop odor notwithstanding.

Joss had bought the farm a year before, kept to himself, didn't have any parties, and didn't borrow any tools. I'd only seen a glimpse of him from a distance and imagined him to be some eccentric hippy, or even worse, a hipster dude getting back to nature. He grew organic vegetables in addition to his free-range chicken business.

Elliott had become a fan of Joss too, although that was probably more about visiting the baby chicks than the farmer himself.

It didn't take long for the traumatized chicken to scurry home, probably to blab to all his chicken friends about the torture he'd endured on his jaunt. The metal gates to the various pens were all locked. How did he get out? I was about to put him back in the closest one but realized he might belong somewhere else, so I went to the front door. Charlie followed along, hopping up the two steps to join me. Then the smart aleck ran across my foot, making me jump a bit, to ring the doorbell before I could. Joss the farmer was lucky enough to have a normal ding-dong doorbell. We both stood and waited.

A man wearing a black T-shirt answered the door with an annoyed expression. Even with the frown, he was attractive, in a non-hippy, non-hipster way. More like a *muscular-guy-who-puts-out-a-fire-and-then-drives-off-on-a-motorcycle* way. He looked from Charlie to me and his expression became confused. "You're not Charlie."

Ah, he must be a constant victim of the button-pushing. "Nope. Charlie rang my doorbell, and I brought him back." I held out my hand and then remembered that they'd been wrist deep in chicken livers. Even though I'd worn gloves to my elbows, it felt inappropriate. I pulled my hand back. "Colbie Summers. I'm, uh, helping out my dad a bit."

He'd reached out to shake my hand and it hung out there, shake-less.

"I've been handling...meat," I explained.

He smiled, as if figuring out I'd been holding chicken parts. "For your cat food business," he said. The wrinkles around his eyes deepened, and I noticed how blue they were.

Whoa. That was a nice smile. "Um, yes," I said, practically stuttering. "This batch is just for taste-testing. Not by me. By Trouble. You know. My cat." Although I had been known to try a few of the recipes. "The food I sell is actually made in a commercial kitchen." *Stop talking*, I told myself. Charlie seemed to lose interest and jumped back down the steps.

"Your dad told me about Trouble," he said, keeping an eye on the chicken. "Sorry about the whole doorbell thing. Charlie was used for some kind of psychology experiments by his previous owner and will poke at anything button-like."

"It's okay," I said.

He shook his head as he came out and closed the door. "I don't know how he gets out all the time. He's the best escape artist I ever had." He walked to the edge of the porch. "It must be the trough. It's too close to the fence but I'd need a crane to move it."

From that viewpoint the farm was picture perfect—its large red barn painted with white trim, a green tractor parked beside old-fashioned gas tanks, and the chickens scratching in the pens. "Sorry," I said. "Don't have one of those with me." I turned to go. "Nice meeting you. Good luck with Charlie." I wasn't going to tell him that I couldn't leave my chicken livers marinating in green curry very long or the flavor would be too intense for my feline customers.

"Nice to meet you," he said. "You want to see the chicks before you rush back?"

"Um…" Was that how a chicken farmer made his move? I did a quick inventory of what I looked like. Cut off shorts to deal with the heat, a Padres Tshirt stained with meat juice, flip-flops, and a rolled-up bandana around my light brown hair with the copper stripe I needed to revive. And, oh yeah, red-rimmed eyes and no makeup. I was definitely safe from any moves by the farmer. And who could resist chicks? "Sure."

He jogged down the porch steps and walked back to the pen, scooping up Charlie as he opened the gate, and setting him down inside a pen by himself. Some chickens in the next section moved closer as if to check out the action. "In here," Joss said.

I walked carefully through the pen, watching where I put my feet. The door to the chicken coop was open and a few birds sat in nests. Then he opened a door inside and we were in some kind of incubator room. An orchestra of chick peeps reached a crescendo and an overwhelming chicken poop scent whooshed by.

"Whoa," I said, plugging my nose and then looking over apologetically.

"Sorry," he said cheerfully. "It takes a little getting used to."

When Joss moved closer, the chirping became even louder.

"So, the chicks love you," I said, not being able to resist the pun.

He looked startled for a second until he realized I was joking. "These are a bit too young for me."

I moved closer to the raised wooden beds with high sides holding the chicks. Heat lamps shone on them, even when it was so hot outside, and the brown and black fuzz balls moved closer to us. "They're adorable," I said. "They don't look like Charlie."

"No," Joss said. "They're Ameraucanas. They lay blue eggs." He picked one up gently. "Here." He put the baby chick in my cupped hands.

I couldn't help but say, "Aw."

And then it pooped. Right in my hand.

"Oops," he said. "Occupational hazard."

And then it pooped again.

"Let me—" he started, and I gladly tipped the chick into his hands. For some reason, I kept my hands together to prevent the mess from escaping, even though there was plenty on the floor.

He gently placed the creature back in its home, and pulled a wet wipe from a handy container hanging high above chicken level by the back door. "Here," he repeated, his eyes laughing at me.

"I got it." I grabbed the wipe, cleaning my hands as quickly as I could. "I'm a mom," I said a little defensively. "A little poop doesn't bother me." Of course, chicken poop was a different story. "I better get back." *To wash my hands with bleach.*

He opened the back door and I walked outside, the sun accosting my eyes again. Then I hit something slimy, sliding a whole two feet and wind-milling my arms before coming to a halt.

I looked down.

A hose had leaked, creating a slimy puddle of mud and chicken poop, which was now slopped all over my flip flops that were pointing in different directions, my feet solidly in the mess.

This time, Joss looked chagrined. "Sorry, sorry. I meant to replace that...." He looked at my feet as if not knowing what to do, and then bit his lip, trying not to smile.

"I'll..." *Burn these* didn't seem nice to say out loud. "Just go..."

"Yeah," he said, valiantly holding back laughter.

Men never outgrow poop humor.

I walked back to my dad's house, futilely attempting to scrape the mess off my flip flops onto the tiny patches of grass that lined the sidewalks. That was sticky stuff.

My dad's street looked like it could be in a seventies sitcom, with neat row houses, all the same white stucco walls and red clay tile roofs. Small driveways led to separate two car garages in the back, usually used for storage or workshops. Every yard hosted a few palm trees and a dried-out lawn that wasn't doing a good job surviving the summer drought regulations. The houses on my dad's side backed up to a huge family farm. The farmer had refused to sell to developers, so my dad had the best of both worlds. The convenience of all things suburbia and a wonderful view of open farmland. Of course, that open farmland smelled strongly of fertilizer at times, but it was worth it.

I tossed my disgusting flip flops and the poop-covered wipe in the garbage and used the garden hose to clean my feet before heading inside.

"Your phone rang," my dad called out from the living room over the sound of *Storage Wars*, his favorite show.

I grabbed my cell and headed back to the stove, tripping over the now-loving cat who wound around my ankles and purred, clearly saying, "*I wuv you so much. Isn't it time to taste test?*"

My Meowio Batali Gourmet Cat Food was marketed as organic food for the discerning cat, and many of my customers welcomed the most exotic of spices. But if Trouble didn't like it, I dropped it. I'd learned early on that she never steered me wrong. If she liked it, it sold. If she didn't like it, other cats didn't either.

My whole business was inspired by Trouble. I'd found her, not even six weeks old, abandoned in an apartment when a tenant skipped out on the rent. Elliott and I immediately fell in love with her tiny orange face and white paws, and adopted her. Because of the splash of white on her chest, Elliott had originally wanted to call her Skimbleshanks, after a cat character in the musical *Cats*.

She'd had a lot of digestive problems, and the only food she could handle was what I made. That, combined with her natural kitten mischievousness, earned her the name Trouble.

Soon, friends started asking to buy little jars of the same food for their cats, which is how I learned that there was a demand for organic, human-grade cat food. I increased my production, cooking at odd hours when I could sneak it in around my job managing the apartment building where we lived.

When I'd tried to expand to farmers' markets, I learned there were a lot of regulations I'd have to follow to make it a real business, including cooking all the food sold at the market in a certified kitchen.

My previous customers still demanded my original products, including the cute packaging, so I spent at least one morning a week indulging them. Their cats had benefitted from me learning how to add vitamins and other goodies to make the food more nutritious.

I'd already been up for hours cooking and packaging my Chicken & Sage Indulgence. The herbal smell bothered Elliott and my dad, so I liked to get the kitchen aired out before they even woke up. Trouble absolutely loved that recipe–she'd come running the moment the sage hit the sizzling olive oil and yelled at me to give her tidbits the whole time I was cooking. When I was done with production, I switched to trying new recipes.

My phone had a message from my best friend, Lani, but I had to finish up the chicken liver curry dish before calling her back. I'd also received an alert that someone had given my business a review on SDHelp. I clicked over to the site and saw that a J. Greene had given me one star!

I opened the app to read the review. *I bought this cat food at the local flea market—*

Flea market? It's a farmers' market, idiot. There's a big difference. I read on.

I had high hopes for this locally-produced, organic cat food, but my cat took one bite and walked away. I couldn't taste it–even I don't love my cat that much–but I sniffed it and it smelled awful. A combination of chemicals and rotten meat. Will never buy again.

What? That was impossible. I'd never had a bad review like this. Once someone complained about the price, but I'd never be able to compete price-wise with the big guys. What should I do? Ignore it? Contact Mr. J. Greene and offer to replace it?

I put a few pieces of curried chicken into the refrigerator to cool while I mentally ran through my process. Since my dad got sick, I hadn't always been in the commercial kitchen the two mornings a week I could afford to rent, relying on my cook who always followed my instructions meticulously. Could something have gone wrong with one batch? But then I would hear from more than one customer. I clicked on the website to see if anyone had left a complaint there. Nothing. I took a deep breath. Maybe it was an isolated incident. Or total bull.

To reassure myself, I turned to the page that had testimonials from my customers. So many of them noted how much healthier their cats were because they ate Meowio food.

"Mom!" Elliott yelled as he ran down the stairs, landing at the bottom with a thud. My son rarely did anything quietly.

I met him in the hall while my dad silenced the TV and stuck his head out to see what was going on.

"I got a callback for Horton!" Elliott announced as he threw his arms in the air in triumph and then fell on the floor in a dramatic faint, clutching his phone to his chest.

"That's awesome," I said, pushing back the guilt that I'd totally forgotten about his audition for theater summer camp. Starting on Monday, he'd be spending two weeks with a bunch of other drama kids on a musical—his idea of heaven. On the last Friday, the whole camp would perform *Seussical the Musical*. "Isn't Horton one of the leads?" The musical incorporated a couple of Dr. Seuss books into one plot including *Horton Hears a Who*.

Elliott rolled himself up and jumped to his feet, his dark brown hair flopping over one eye. "Yes!"

"Congratulations, kid," I said, delighted for him. "When's the audition?"

He clicked on his phone, reading farther down the email he'd received. His face fell. "Uh-oh," he said. "It's this Thursday afternoon."

That was one of my farmers' market days and my biggest sales day. My best customers knew they could find me every Thursday afternoon in downtown San Diego, selling my cat food with Trouble watching over the booth in her little chef hat. I'd already paid for my prime spot.

I forced a smile. "It's okay," I said. "We'll just go to the market late."

"I can take him," my dad called out from the living room.

Elliott's eyes widened and he shook his head in a silent plea.

Oh man. I had to handle this carefully. "It's okay, Dad. I love going to Elliott's auditions," I said in a light tone. "And he can help me at the market afterward."

He subsided with a "harrumph." Normally having my dad drive Elliott might work, but he hadn't driven much since he got out of the hospital. And this was Elliott's first time auditioning for the Sunnyside Junior Theater, and he didn't know anyone. Even when Elliott tried out for his old theater group where he felt comfortable, he had to be managed carefully so he went into his audition feeling confident. And my dad hadn't been very supportive of anything Elliott did that wasn't sports-related.

Elliott let out his breath. He and my dad had gotten along on our short visits over the years, but hadn't found much common ground since we'd moved in. My dad wouldn't admit to needing help after his second devastating bout with pneumonia. My macho, football-playing father hated being weak and being forced to accept support from the same daughter he'd driven out of the house thirteen years ago.

And he wouldn't say it out loud, but it was clear he wasn't happy with Elliott's fashion choices. Especially the way Elliott shaved one side of his head and allowed the other to grow long. From the photos of my own grunge days in high school, I knew Elliott would regret that look in the future, but he had to make his own fashion mistakes.

"The director sent me the sheet music for 'Alone in the Universe,' and I only have two days to learn it. I'm gonna go practice." Elliott ran back up to his room, taking the stairs a couple at a time.

"Break a leg!" I called after him. I smiled, caught up in his enthusiasm. Until my dad "harrumphed" again from the living room.

I took a deep breath, determined to let my dad's bad attitude go. *He's sick*, I told myself and headed back to the kitchen.

But he didn't stop. "I don't know why you let him do that nonsense," he said, lighting my simmering anger.

I did a U-turn at the kitchen doorway and stomped into the living room. "What nonsense? Having fun with other kids? Developing his talents? Pursuing a dream?"

My dad scowled. "Singing and dancing's not preparing him for the future."

"He's twelve, Dad," I said sarcastically. "He has time. And you think playing with a ball on a field prepares him for the future?"

"It sure does," he said, defensive. "It teaches teamwork. And following the rules. Something both of ya could learn." He sat back in his chair, and suddenly he seemed smaller in it. Had he lost more weight?

My anger washed out of me. "He loves it, Dad," I said, my voice calmer. "And there's a heck of a lot of teamwork going on behind the scenes and on stage." I'd seen it first-hand during the obligatory volunteering that went along with any kind of youth theater.

He narrowed his eyes, as if trying to figure out if I was just feeling sorry for him. Then he turned the TV sound back on with his remote. *Storage Wars* characters were trying to goad each other into bidding higher on someone's junk.

"It's a good thing my investments are paying off so I can help with his college," he grumbled as I took a step to the door. "My new fund is up a full twenty percent this month."

"What?" I asked. "You have investments?"

"Of course I have investments," he said, bristling again. "You think I'm an idiot?"

"No," I said. I couldn't imagine having enough money for "investments."

"You're helping with Elliott's college?"

"Of course I am," he said. "He's not getting a singing scholarship, is he?"

I gaped at him. That comment had so many levels of insult that I couldn't think of a retort to cover them all.

Luckily my phone rang before any sound could come out of my mouth. I counted to ten on the way back to the kitchen and answered it.

"Oh. My. God," Lani said, her voice breaking up a little over her car Bluetooth connection. "I'm gonna kill Piper."

"Good morning to you too," I said. Piper was her wife and Lani threatened to kill her about once a week, usually for no good reason.

I pulled out the now cool pieces of chicken curry and put them in Trouble's dish. She sniffed it, and then took a bite. Her lips curled back as she chewed. Then she spit it out.

Shoot. There goes that recipe. Unless I tried it again with less curry?

"She threw out my latest prototype! On purpose!" I heard Lani's car engine zoom in the background, as if it was angry at Piper too.

Lani was the owner and creator of Find Your Re-Purpose, an online boutique of unique baby fashions recycled from used clothing. She cut up old clothing, sewed different materials together, added some fabric paint or other touches, and voila! A beautiful, one-of-a-kind, hundred dollar outfit that anyone with too much money could buy for a baby who would most likely spit up on it in less than five minutes.

We'd met years before when she was the costume designer for one of Elliott's plays, and quickly figured out that she lived in my dad's neighborhood. After a few sleepless nights of last minute costume adjustments before the show's opening, we'd become best friends.

"Was it that cape idea you were kicking around?" I asked.

"Yes!" she said. "It was the cutest thing EV-ER!"

I'd had my own doubts about the safety of capes for infants, but had kept them to myself. Since Piper was a pediatrician, I knew she'd step in. "Where are you headed?" I asked, trying to distract her.

"Ventura," she said. "A thrift shop just got a big donation of clothes from a rich European family who spent the last six months in Malibu. The material has a bunch of cool designs the shop owner has never seen before so he put them aside for me. I can't wait to see them."

Ventura was almost four hours from Sunnyside, which meant Lani would be gone most of the day. Since she liked company on her trip, I put her on speaker phone right by the stove, resumed my stirring, and settled in for a long conversation.

"Have you heard from Twomey's yet?" she asked, with a change in her tone that meant *now-it's-time-for-friendly-nagging*. She'd encouraged me to contact the local chain of seven organic food stores offering my cat food products.

"Not yet," I admitted. In my e-mail, I'd pushed the fact that buying local was all the rage, especially for the kind of people who bought organic products to help save the planet.

Seeing Meowio Batali products on the shelves of that many stores would be a dream come true. But I wasn't sure how I'd meet any significant increase in demand without hiring more people. And that took money.

I was pretty stretched already—both physically and money-wise. Too bad cloning me wasn't an option yet. If I had two, maybe three more of me, I could do everything I should be doing.

I changed the subject. "Hey, I finally met my neighbor."

"That cute chicken farmer?" she asked.

I turned on the frying pan and dribbled in extra virgin olive oil. "How'd you know he was cute?"

"Everyone knows he's cute," she said. "He's also single, keeps to himself and hasn't dated at all."

"Good to know," I said. I told her all about the chicks and the unfortunate poop incident.

"That's such a meet cute!" she said. "You can tell your grandchildren that story where you fell in love with his chicks first."

"I think if there's poop involved, it's the exact opposite of a meet cute," I said. "And I really don't have time to date right now."

"You know, it's really a little like Romeo and Juliet, except with your cat and chickens," she said. "Joss is a Montague and you're the Cat-ulets." She giggled at her own joke.

"And you know how they ended up." I tossed chunks of chicken in the pan. "Hey, did you head out of town on purpose so I couldn't drag you to my Power Moms trade show?"

"Oh yeah," she said unapologetically. "It's the only reason I chose today to drive to freakin' Ventura. Just to get away from your cult."

I laughed. The Sunnyside Power Moms, or SPMs for short, was a group of home business owners who worked together to network and support each other. Our leader, Twila Jenkins, got the idea to start the group when the third mom came up to her at the Sunnyside Elementary School playground to invite her to a party at her house. One of those "parties" where the host/salesperson puts out lovely hors d'oeuvres and lots of wine so that her guests, i.e., sales targets, will feel more inclined to buy thirty dollar candles and forty-five dollar candle holders.

Twila had invited me to join after learning about my cat food business.

"You'll come around," I said. "The first step was when you suggested your friend Fawn become an SPM. You're one step closer to becoming One of Us. One of Us." I chanted that in a low tone a few times until she interrupted me.

"Not a chance," she said. "Hey! You should manufacture some kind of scandal. That'll get people interested in your little coven."

I rolled my eyes, even though she couldn't see me. "Be nice or I'll sign you up to host a candle party at your house."

She gasped dramatically. "A fate worse than death."